Revenge of Cleotina

Holly Hamilton

Ukiyoto Publishing

All global publishing rights are held by

Ukiyoto Publishing

Published in 2024

Content Copyright © Holly Hamilton

ISBN 9789362697776

All rights reserved.

No part of this publication may be reproduced, transmitted, or stored in a retrieval system, in any form by any means, electronic, mechanical, photocopying, recording or otherwise, without the prior permission of the publisher.

The moral rights of the author have been asserted.

This work blends fact and fiction. While some elements may be inspired by real-life events, names, characters, businesses, places, locales, and incidents have been created by the author's imagination or utilised fictitiously. Any resemblance to actual persons, living or dead, or actual events may exist but is not indicative of a direct correlation.

This book is sold subject to the condition that it shall not by way of trade or otherwise, be lent, resold, hired out or otherwise circulated, without the publisher's prior consent, in any form of binding or cover other than that in which it is published.

www.ukiyoto.com

Contents

Chapter 1: The Library (Kira's POV)	1
Chapter 2: What Happened Long Ago (Cleotina's POV)	4
Chapter 3: Upper Egypt (Cleotina's POV)	8
Chapter 4: Nephthys (Cleotina's POV)	11
Chapter 5: The Mysterious Museum (Kira's POV)	14
Chapter 6: The Banquet (Cleotina's POV)	17
Chapter 7: Mourning Nebetta (Cleotina's POV)	20
Chapter 8: Dr. Sawyer (Kira's POV)	24
Chapter 9: Time Travel (Kira's POV)	28
Chapter 10: A Selfish Pharoah (Cleotina's POV)	31
Chapter 11: In Time with Alex Sawyer (Kira's POV)	34
Chapter 12: We Are Family (Cleotina's POV)	38
Chapter 13: Observing the Past (Kira's POV)	40
Chapter 14: For Ay's Pleasure (Cleotina's POV)	45
Chapter 15: Confused About Alex (Kira's POV)	50
Chapter 16: Ay Returns (Cleotina's POV)	53
Chapter 17: Home Sick (Kira's POV)	57
Chapter 18: Remember the Mission (Cleotina's POV)	61
Chapter 19: The Shining Star (Cleotina's POV)	64
Chapter 20: Death of a Pharoah (Cleotina's POV)	67
Chapter 21: Learning from History (Kira's POV)	70
About the Author	*73*

Chapter 1: The Library (Kira's POV)

The present:

"Kira, you don't have to get so butt hurt about a writing assignment. It's a research paper on King Tut. So why were you being such a bitch in class today? The professor almost asked you to leave."

Maybe it's not my place to correct history, but I know the truth about how King Tut died in my bones.

"King Tut didn't die from a chariot racing accident or a fight to the death. My ancestor, Cleotina, murdered him, and I'm going to prove it."

My high heels click the sidewalk. I pull my backpack strap over my shoulder and head toward the library.

"Kira, where are you going? Hey, wait, come back," Asher shouts.

Asher's been my boyfriend since high school. He knows me better than anyone. But today, I am more interested in research and history than an excellent make-out sesh.

The library steps ascend toward the large brick building. The architecture resembles famous cathedrals from Paris. The brick on the building is faded with greys and browns.

The librarian sits toward the front of the library. Her round glasses and frizzy blonde hair tell me her story that she is a woman who is determined to research and help others do so.

"Excuse me. I am looking for the Egyptology section."

She puts her book down and places a bookmark within the pages. The librarian would call me a book murderer if she knew I bent the pages to mark my place in a novel.

"Upstairs on the third floor. It's near the fireplace. You can't miss it."

She continues reading and leaves me to my own devices. Then, finally, I take the elevator to the third floor and find the fireplace.

I find the E-section along the wall and start searching for anything I can find on King Tut.

"If you're here to do Professor Chang's King Tut paper, don't bother. These books are either picked over or are a complete waste of time. Instead, I suggest you find a museum and do your research there. It would be a much better paper, don't you think?"

A young man with black head buds in his ears says to me.

"I'd like to try my research from the library first, thanks. I am going to prove Professor Chang wrong," I say as I tighten my fist.

"What are you going to prove him wrong about? It's a paper on how King Tut died. There isn't much to tell other than what's been discovered by archeologists and recorded in history books."

"Ugh, not you too. I am going to prove that my ancestor murdered King Tut. This paper means everything to me. So, if you'd excuse me, I have research to do on Cleotina."

I turn away from the young man and start looking for anything the books have on my ancestor.

"Did you say, Cleotina? Was your ancestor Cleotina? Hmmm, that's interesting. I suggest you go to the museum then and ask to speak to Dr. Sawyer. He may have the answers you are looking for. I heard he's recently returned from Egypt with papyrus scrolls mentioning a Cleotina. If she really is your relative, you are not going to find your answers here at this crummy university library."

The young man seems to know his way around this subject.

"How do you know so much about Egypt? How can I trust you?"

"Because Dr. Sawyer is my father, just tell him Alex sent you," Alex says as he shows me his identification card. The card says 'Alexander Sawyer.'

"Thanks. I'm Kira, by the way. Which museum is it," I ask, wondering if this is too blunt of me.

"The Field Museum in Chicago. I can take you if you'd like. My dad will understand. What's your real name," Alex asks as he tilts his glasses back toward his nose.

"Kira."

"And that's short for?" Alex knows my first name is a nickname. Not even my boyfriend knows that.

"Neferekira."

"Like the pharaohs. Yes, my dad will definitely want to speak with someone with your ancestry."

Alex stands up and packs his backpack. He grabs my hand and takes me to the elevator. I leave the library without any books or research to back me up.

"Why are we leaving the library? How do I know I can trust you?"

I follow Alex to the parking lot, and he opens the passenger door for me.

"Don't you want to find out the truth? Isn't it time the world knows the truth about why King Tut died at the young age of nineteen? He was our age when he died. It's not only about his death. Don't you want to know how he lived?"

I get into the passenger seat as Alex closes the door behind me. I don't usually get in cars with strangers, but if my gut tells me to follow Alex, I know it's the right thing to do. I want to be on the right side of history and discover for myself if my ancestor is the murderer that my great grandma described Cleotina to be.

Time to start speaking to me from your grave, Cleotina. Because your legacy is about to be put on trial.

Chapter 2: What Happened Long Ago (Cleotina's POV)

The past:

"Slow down, Cleotina. Today is your selection day. You're going to have to be on your best behavior," the mother says as she grabs my hand and walks me to the bed of our tiny house. This morning, the dirt floor is extra dry, and the air is hot. Egypt is hot and sweat pushes my makeup toward the ground.

"I don't care about being selected. Why can't the Pharaoh collect other women from other countries for his play collection?" My words are harsh, and I snap at my mother like a poisonous viper. It's not her fault our culture is the way it is. Women aren't really seen. We are there to produce heirs, honor the gods, and serve the pharaohs. So, the noblest thing I can do is be selected by the Pharaoh.

"Gyasi, come here and tell your sister to behave. She won't listen to me," mother demands as she finishes brushing my hair and painting eye makeup against my eyes. Our eyeliner looks like hieroglyphs. It's forbidden to explore the tombs of the great kings, but I have anyway. Gyasi, my brother, once guarded the graves to protect the treasures of the pharaohs' past. But not anymore. He was injured by a lion and barely made it back alive. He limps now and has been sent back to spend the rest of his days with his family.

Gyasi is proud of his former life and speaks of it often. It's no wonder mother named him 'wonderful' in the common tongue called Coptic. Back when I was still a child, Gyasi snuck me into the great pyramid and showed me the hieroglyphs. All the noble families learned to read and write. I was above the poorer women in our community in lower Egypt. But we all knew that being noble meant the selection would sneak up on us one day when we'd least expect it.

"Cleotina, you have to listen to mother. You have to lower your eyes, kneel when asked, and pray to Thoth for wisdom. If you are selected, there is something I am going to need you to do. You know what, never mind, forget I said anything."

Gyasi gets off my bed and forms a first with his knuckles. He cracks the air between his tan fingers and clears his throat. His brown eyes shift away from me, and I don't have it in me to press the news out of his further. There is no point. When Gyasi wants to speak, he will when he is ready.

"I'm excited, Gyasi. If I am selected, I will get to see Nebetta again. Since the day she was selected, I haven't seen her in five years. I know you had affection toward her. Have you seen her since the Pharaoh selected her to be a part of his harem?"

Gyasi turns around, and his body is tense like a thousand horses getting pulled back by their reigns. His eyes speak of war and death.

"Cleotina, there's something I need to tell you. Nebetta was put to death two weeks ago. She was accused of stealing the royal crown jewels. The Pharoah ended her life. You will see Nebetta in the afterlife. She is safe now with Osiris. Only the God of the underworld knows where her soul dwells now. I wanted to ask something of you, and I know you will say yes. Can you pray to Petbe tonight? He is the only God I care about now."

Petbe is the God of revenge, and the last time my brother prayed to Petbe, he was attacked by a lion the next day.

"No, brother. I can't pray to Petbe for you. But I will act on his behalf for you if the gods will it."

Gyasi takes my hands and leads me out of the house. The horses for the selection have arrived at our door. A man with a piece of parchment jumps off the back of a black stallion. Enslaved people gather around him and give him shade beneath a large palm branch.

"Cleotina, daughter of Ammon, sister of the honorable Gyasi, and blessed child of Isis, you have been summoned to the palace by decree of Pharaoh Tutankhamun. Upon arrival, you will begin your selection phase and will be tested. If you pass the test and are selected, you will have the honor of pleasing his royal highness whenever he calls upon you. If you are not selected, another position may be selected for you. To pass the selection process, we suggest you don't speak unless spoken to; otherwise, the same fate that your friend Nebetta suffered will fall upon you. So, gather your things, and get on the horse at high noon."

I kneel at the messenger and don't show any sign of emotion. I am a woman, and feelings don't exist. But inside, I am screaming, screaming to pass the selection so I can put a knife into the Pharaoh that ended my best friend, Nebetta's life.

Oh god, Petbe, I call upon you to help me avenge my friends' life so that she will find comfort in the underworld with Osiris.

I make my vow before Ra, the Sun God, that before the Pharaoh's next birthday, he will be walking beneath the darkness of death with his throat in Anubis' mouth.

I return to my house, and Gyasi finds me. I pack my favorite dresses, makeup, and a knife that will help me end that demon's life. Gyasi pulls the knife out of my bag and shakes his head.

"What are you doing? You can't bring this to the palace. They will hang you as a traitor. You will have your chance for revenge, but don't do it this way. Take your time and study the King. I am upset about Nebetta, too. She is the only woman I ever loved. I wanted to marry her, but the Pharoah beat me to it. The King always gets what he wants. It's our job to obey on the surface and plot in the blackness of night. If you are going to kill him, sister, make him fall in love with you first and then kill him when everyone turns away. He will call you to his chambers after you are selected. You can get to know him then. Learn his ways and make sure nobody is watching. Then, when it's your turn, kill him with this," Gyasi says.

He puts a sharp knife in my hair. It looks like a hairpin but is a dagger hidden beneath the blackness of my hair.

"I will, brother. I will end that bastard pharaoh for our Nebetta. You have my word."

I pick up my bags and hug my brother Gyasi one last time, knowing that Petbe, the God of revenge, is already answering my prayers.

Chapter 3: Upper Egypt (Cleotina's POV)

The past:

The ride to Upper Egypt smells like sweat and tastes like salt. My neck is hot, and the sweat falls down my hair, making it frizz out in all directions. I have been selected to pleasure the Pharaoh. He will take away all our virginities and decide who is best at having sex and who isn't. Those who pass will be brought to the palace and will be educated in the ways of Ra.

There is no romance in the land of tears. No romance in pleasuring a king I have only seen once. There are no dreams when my nightmares have woken up. Only the god Petbe will guide my thoughts. Thoth no longer has the wisdom to pass to me. I hope his temples burn and catch fire tonight.

The palace gets larger and vaster as we approach. The columns are tall, and the pillars are wide. As far as the eye can see, hieroglyphs tell our story and sing our songs. They will be there for ancestors to remember us by. By the time history discovers my story, it will remember my purpose is to take out the young Pharaoh. I haven't seen him since he was a boy. His father, Pharaoh Akhenaten died, and Tutankhamun became Pharaoh at the age of eight. He didn't know how to rule his people, and the only thing mesmerizing about him was his brown eyes.

No eye color in the world will change the fate of the Pharaoh. I will murder him after I get to know him. It's just as Gyasi said, I must learn about him and gain his trust. It is all an act. Everything I do, say, and breathe will be to please a man who doesn't deserve to live. Nebetta, you will see the Pharaoh soon, and Osiris will help you destroy his soul.

When Tutankhamun perishes, and they build monuments of him, I will personally defile his face. It's the most treasonous act I can perform. To spoil his image means he won't have a peaceful afterlife. And why should Tutankmun rest in peace when Nebetta was sentenced to death by his very voice?

The palace gates part and the chariots carry us into the following chapters of our lives. A sea of hundreds of women are brought to a large room. We are all similar in height, status, and physical features. Some are prettier than others, but we all know the horrible truth that out of the five hundred women here today, only twenty-five will be selected for the Pharaoh's harem. The other four-hundred and seventy-five will either be married off, turned into servants, or sent to temples to serve as priestesses. A few might even be put to death if they look the wrong way or don't cooperate.

Back at home, I did what I wanted and said my feelings. But here in the palace, I keep to myself. There are no friends when death is on the line. My eye-make-up still resides on my face as Pharaoh is called to look upon the plethora of women.

The selection process is long and uncomfortable. We strip our wardrobe, and they feel every inch of our bodies. Our breasts are compared. Our womanhood is exposed for the men to fondle and make notes of. I think about my mission and let them touch me where they want. My robes are removed as I lay eyes on Pharaoh Tutankhamun. His brown eyes are still as mesmerizing as the last time I saw them. The light brown eyes scan my body, and he whispers into his advisor's ears. His chief advisor is a fearless man named Ay. The other advisor's name is Horemheb. I wait for the servants to put my wardrobe back on me. Tutankhamun whispers to both of them, and I stand as tall as I can.

"His Royal Highness, Tutankhamun, would like to know your name."

"My name is Cleotina, my king," I bow on my knees to show respect to a man who deserves death.

"I remember you, Cleotina. It's your smile that gives you away. I hope you make it past the selection process. In fact, I insist upon it," Tutankhamun says.

Ay and Horemheb whispers to the Pharaoh and look back at me.

"The king has decided to expedite your selection process. Therefore, you will be properly dressed and will join him for dinner at the palace this evening. The Pharaoh may call upon you if you pass tonight's dinner banquet."

The Pharaoh has called me by name. Being the most desired woman in lower Egypt has given me an advantage after all. My reputation has made it to the ears of King Tutankhamun. My brother, Gyasi, would be proud of my progress here today. But, despite my naked body and the thousands of men touching me and inspecting me, it is the Pharaoh who is impressed.

King Tutankhamun reaches his hand out to me as the servants finish putting on the remainder of my gown. He whispers something into my ear, and I am keen to keep it to myself.

"Welcome to my harem." I blush a little but try not to smile from ear to ear. As charming as King Tutankhamun is, he will not get me to fall for him. I made a pack with the god Petbe to seek revenge and avenge Nebetta. I will.

Chapter 4: Nephthys (Cleotina's POV)

The past.

"This way, Cleotina," an older lady servant grabs me by the hand and leads me to a bath. My gown is removed again. I will never get used to being naked in front of strangers, but it is something I must pretend to enjoy if I am to survive the customs of palace culture.

"What is your name?"

"My name is Nephthys. You may call me Neph if you'd like. From now on, I will tend to your needs. I will teach you how to dress, sit, and stand in the palace during your selection phase. I will say, my dear, the Pharaoh is very pleased with you. If you act the way you're supposed to, he may add you to his collection yet."

Nephthys leads me down a large corridor that takes me deeper and deeper into the maze of the palace. It will take me eons to learn my way around here and learn it I shall if I am to kill the Pharaoh and run away from his body in time.

"He's quite handsome, isn't he?" I don't know what to say. My opinions were supposed to be left at the door. But if I praise his Highness to everyone and defend his honor with my words, that will surely give me a better chance of joining his harem of pleasure.

"It's not my place or your place to say. But I believe most women think so. I've heard he is very good at pleasuring women. The ladies in his harem have been known to blush from ear to ear. But that's just palace gossip. So, what does an old lady like me know about pleasuring the Pharaoh?"

"Were you ever in the harem yourself? For Tutankhamun's father?"

Nephthys brushes my hair and scrubs every inch of me. She tells me about Pharaoh Akhenaten and how he changed the religion of Egypt. During his reign, he decided to make Egypt monotheistic. The priests didn't like that very much and wanted to worship all the gods. Eventually, after his death, Tutankhamun changed the religion back to the way it was supposed to be. It is why he is a famous king.

"Is he a kind man?" Maybe I am not supposed to ask these types of questions. But I want to know what I am getting myself into.

Nephthys takes a rag and rings it out in the water. Then, she lathers my back in soap and scrubs it off.

"He is a much kinder king than his father was. I will say, miss. I am sorry to hear about your friend, Nebetta."

My body tightens, and my jaws come together. She puts her hand on my shoulder.

"How do you know about that?"

"I've been told to keep an eye on you. They want to make sure you are kept in line. They see your relationship with Nebetta as an emotional weakness. But I think they are wrong. What they did to that girl is unforgivable. It's not my place to judge."

I squeeze Nephthys's hand, and I now realize that she will be the only friend I make within the palace walls.

"Thanks for your sympathies. I do miss her. But I want to try my best to get past it and join his majesty's harem."

I don't want to be a suspect. It's too early for that. Nebetta's death is the reason I am here.

"I will still keep my eyes on you, girl. But don't worry. I will ensure you are selected for his majesty's harem. You have already made an impression. Let's not keep them waiting time to get you changed. I have a wonderful purple gown that will make your green eyes shine. I've never seen such eyes in Egypt. The gods have blessed your face. No wonder he has taken a liking to you."

Nephthys takes my hand and helps me out of the bath. She gives me a towel, and I dry myself off. The purple gown flows to my feet. Golden bracelets are placed on my wrists, and a veil covers my face. Until the selection process is complete, no man is allowed to see my entire face—only the Pharaoh. When I eat, I must keep my chewing under the veil. I belong to the Pharaoh now. Until he approves of us, all five-hundred women are to be kept this way. I cover my face and prepare for the dinner banquet at hand.

Chapter 5: The Mysterious Museum (Kira's POV)

The present.

Alex Sawyer is a mystery. He hasn't said anything to me since our drive to the museum began. It's late, and the drive is longer than I thought it was.

"So, are you dating that Asher guy?" The way he asks it rubs me the wrong way.

"Yeah, he's my high school sweetheart. Why do you ask?" Alex's demeanor and the way he stops the car to look at me tell me he has more on his mind than being on the right side of history.

"You might want to dump him. He's not the right guy for you. We're here."

I don't have time to reply to this wayward conversation. However, Alex's mystery makes him quite creepy and charming at the same time. Should I let myself flirt with him? Would I get more answers about the past if I did?

The museum looks like the Abraham Lincoln Memorial. It has many columns and steps going into the main building. But this is nighttime, and Alex knows his way to all the secret entrances the general public doesn't know about.

A security guard stops us, and Alex shows him his pass.

"Hello, Alex. Your father is working on the scrolls he's discovered on his recent travels. Unfortunately, I can't allow you to bring strangers to the museum this late at night."

Alex whispers something to the guard, and they let me through. The guard checks me with a metal detector. This is starting to feel more and more like an airport inspection.

Alex grabs my hand, and as his father looks up at us from his desk. Alex kisses the side of my cheek.

"Play along," Alex whispers. Alex grabs my hand, and I hold his back. I am not comfortable cheating on Asher, but if it helps me discover the truth about Cleotina, then I have to do it. Alex isn't terrible looking. In his own way, he is rather handsome.

"Hello, Alex. Who is this young lady? I don't remember you spending time with girls."

"This is my girlfriend, Kira," Alex says as I go and shake his father's hand.

"Dr. Sawyer, it's nice to meet you. My full name is Neferekira, but you can call me Kira."

"Are you Egyptian? What a fascinating name you have, my dear."

"That's why we are here, father, my girlfriend, Kira is a descendant of Cleotina."

Alex squeezes my hand tighter, and I blush. How pathetic I don't even know this guy, and his mysterious ways have attracted me.

"Yes, I believe I am Egyptian in my bloodline. Cleotina is my ancestor, and I believe she murdered King Tutankhamun."

Dr. Sawyer's mouth turns into a smile. He takes us to the papyrus scrolls he discovered.

"Let me show you what I found during my travels to Egypt. King Tut selected your ancestor to serve him in his harem. She lived there with a servant named Nephthys. We know that shortly after King Tut died, Cleotina is no longer mentioned in the scrolls. They believe she fell in love with him. We also found these golden bracelets with her name and the Pharaoh's carved on the inside. I believe they were lovers. But what became of her, I don't know yet. Upon examining King Tut's body at the Cairo Museum, it was concluded that he either died of malaria, a chariot accident, or poor genetics. We will never know for sure, but they recently discovered another possibility. A dagger that would have been kept in someone's hair was found with his burial possessions. It went unnoticed by Howard Carter, the original founder of King Tut's royal tomb. It was inside a box and was buried in his tomb," Dr. Sawyer says.

Alex continues to hold my hand as Dr. Sawyer studies my face.

"You have such fascinating eyes, my dear. For someone of Egyptian blood, they are sure a deep green color," Dr. Sawyer says.

"Thanks, sir. These green eyes have been passed in my family for thousands of years," I reply, wondering if I shouldn't have mentioned that. Cleotina was said to have emerald-green eyes, and if I am her ancestor, having the same eyes as her is remarkable.

"Her eyes are why I fell in love with her," Alex says as he spins me around and puts his lips on mine.

When Alex asked me to play along, I thought he meant with words only and that his kiss on my cheek was a kind gesture. However, it's clear that his intentions are more than just research based. As Alex pulls away, I pull him in for one more kiss and know that Asher will dump me if he ever finds out.

Chapter 6: The Banquet (Cleotina's POV)

The past:

My purple gown is the talk of the banquet. Nephthys is pleased with her handy work. She presents me proudly to Ay, the chief advisor to the King.

"You look stunning, my dear girl. Don't forget to bow and only talk when the King asks you questions. Keep your face covered at all times. Only your eyes can be viewed by everyone. If the Pharaoh selects you for his harem, your face covering can be removed. It's a shame your friend, Nebetta, couldn't be here with us tonight. She would have enjoyed seeing her friend act so lovely. But don't worry, her death was slow and painful. I made sure of that. We all did, didn't we, Horemheb?"

Horemheb smiles and pounds his fist into his other palm. He cracks his knuckles to intimidate me. They intend to make my emotions take over. I can't let that happen.

"I am glad to hear you took such good care of her, my lord. I will see her again someday."

I bow at Ay and Horemheb. What if I am taking revenge on the wrong person? Did the King command Nebetta to be put to death? Or was it Ay and Horemheb's doing? I will never know unless I play my cards right and show respect at all times.

I grab Ay's arm and pretend he is my father taking me to a religious ceremony. It makes the trauma of our conversation disappear into thin air.

"You are very convincing, my dear. Perhaps you deserve to be selected for Pharaoh's harem after all. I will walk you to your seat beside the King. And remember, only answer his questions."

I wave at the crowds and pass the entertainers dancing in the middle of the long banquet hall.

King Tutankhamun rises to greet us and takes my hand. His touch is more comforting than Ay's.

"It's good to see you, Cleotina. I hope you are enjoying yourself?"

"Yes, my lord. It is a magnificent event honoring the gods." I bow low to the ground and kiss his hand on my way up from the floor.

"Your eyes are gorgeous. I am sure all the men in lower Egypt have told you so. Rumors of your beauty reached my ears, and I just had to see for myself if what they say is true. Is it true?"

"It is not for me to say, my lord. That is for you to decide and for me to agree with."

Pharaoh Tutankhamun whispers something into my ear.

"You don't have to be so polite with me. When the banquet is over, I'd like to talk with you alone in private."

"Yes, your grace." I don't want to be alone with the King. His light brown eyes convince me otherwise. They are unique and otherworldly. No wonder rumors of his sexual prowess have reached the ears of my maidservant, Nephthys. He is handsome and somewhat gentle. Did he order men to kill Nebetta, or was it all a lie to test my emotions?

During the banquet, noblemen and commoners pay their taxes to the King. They bow and present their treasures in a powerful lineup. I smile at the King, and my thoughts betray me that the rumors about him in Lower Egypt aren't true. He isn't a vicious monster who hates his people. He is a fair and wise king. I must continue to observe the King and make sure I am not a fool in the process.

The Pharaoh greets his subjects with care and respect. His smile makes his eyes more inviting. Their light brown hues soften when he laughs. The King that my brother, Gyasi, wanted to murder is not the Pharaoh I see before me. But, if I am not careful, his charm might impact me and my mission.

The servants bring out their food. There are quails and all kinds of fruits for the Pharaoh to choose from.

"I have something for you, Cleotina." A servant bows toward me and holds up a small box.

"Open it, " Tutankhamun says. So, I open it and am presented with a golden necklace with a cat charm dangling on the chain. The cat head has two emerald eyes, which resemble the color of my own eyes.

"Thank you, it is beautiful," I say, playing along. But unfortunately, his flattering is making me feel uneasy.

"I knew you would like it. It belonged to your friend Nebetta. The gods rest her soul. When I saw your eye color, I knew you were meant to have it."

Pharaoh has uttered her name in my presence, and no amount of charm can convince me that he isn't guilty. A moment ago, I thought he was a gentle Pharaoh. But now I see him for what he truly is, a monster like Ay and Horemheb. I can't trust any of them, and if Petbe is listening, I hope avenging Nebetta comes sooner rather than later.

Chapter 7: Mourning Nebetta (Cleotina's POV)

The past:

The Pharaoh is a fool. I follow him and hold Nebetta's bracelet in my hands. It's all I have left. I bite the insides of my cheeks the way I did when I was a little girl all those years ago. When Gyasi would tease me in front of all our friends, I would cower behind the large bush in our backyard. Nebetta found me. We were ten years old at the time. She offered me a sip of her water, and we threw rocks by the stream in our free time. We would chase birds and gossip about boys. As we grew older, Nebetta's woman shape developed before mine. Gyasi noticed, and I often embarrassed him in front of his own friends while flirting with them in the process. Flirting came at a significant cost, my father's lecture and the disapproval of my mother. I don't know which of them I feared the most.

Nebetta's bracelet holds her soul in its golden curves. I carry the last of her, and when no one is looking, I will give what is left of Nebetta a proper burial. I don't know where they keep the bodies of alleged traitors. But her memory must live on for the gods to find. If my mother knew of my intentions to steal a Royal artifact for burial, she would disapprove the way she disapproves of everything I have ever done.

My quick tongue is a harsh whip back home in the comforts of the lower Egyptian sun. The land of the Pharaohs is no place for convenience, no place for love, and no place for me. How can I be expected to lie with a man that has no soul? The Pharoah is a selfish man, who takes what he wants, and pretends to be a god. If he were a god, he would sense my emotional need for revenge. I would rather die and see Nebetta in the afterlife than spend a night giving myself away to a horny man.

My thoughts would also be the end of me. Ay and Horemheb are testing my very existence, and even the very Pharoah I was sent to kill is testing me too. By the time I pass the test, as I am sure I will, I will have to kill him before he kills me. There is no way around it now. He dangles her death in front of me. Does it give him pleasure to taunt his subjects with his vial tongue? His very breath gives me offense, and there is nothing I can do in this moment but pretend I am in love with him like all the other women who suck up to the one they call Pharoah. Petbe is with me. I can feel his aura hovering above me like a mighty cloud drifting with the skies.

"This way, my lady," Pharoah Tutankhamun says. The guards follow us, and I remember the knife pin in my hair. I have had to hide it from all of them, even my servant, Nephthys. I want to believe the Nephthys has my best interest at heart, but like the rest of the women who are here, she could be put to death for any reason, at any hour. Death is fragile here in the land of the gods. The son of Ra is all-knowing, and to question him is certain death.

I follow the Pharoah down the long corridor and past the large columns. Large columns are everywhere around the palace. They are a symbol of his divine right to rule and be worshipped. I hold Pharoah's hand, and I see a familiar face as I do. One I have not laid eyes on in the longest of times, Abasi.

The day Nebetta and I met, she found me behind the bushes of my Lower Egyptian home. I met her brother, Abasi. I forgot that he was sent to the palace when he was ten. I hadn't seen him since I was nine, but I knew it was him. He and Nebetta shared the same eyes, and now that she is dead, knowing he is within the palace walls is a comfort. Pharoah catches us exchanging glances.

"Do you two know each other," Pharaoh Tutankhamun asks? If I tell the Pharaoh the truth, he will rub Nebetta's death in his face, and that's the last thing Abasi needs.

"No, I thought he was someone, I know, but I am wrong, my lord," I reply as Abasi stops looking at me. Our contact will be limited, and if we are caught in our lie, we both know the consequences. But there is hope again, now that I know that I have a friend within the walls of the palace. A true friend, who would keep all my secrets, and who also has a reason to end the spoiled brat Pharaoh who stands before me now.

Abasi bows to the Pharaoh as we carry on our way. Abasi knows why I am here. I have been called to impress the Pharaoh and join his hall of harlots. The highest honor is nothing more than a whore house. The world of sex is only enjoyed by those who are male. To be a woman is to be property unless you carry the royal blood of kings in your veins. Even as a nobleman's daughter, my tongue betrays me and is the reason my father almost banished me. It was kept a secret, and it's a good thing too. Otherwise, I would not be in the Pharoah's presence and seek his favor.

We enter the Pharoah's chambers, and the guards are commanded to leave. It astonishes me that the Pharoah can claim a room, demand taxes, and call himself a god. I don't care how amazing he is in bed. No amount of male prowess will ever impress me. The door to his chambers closes, and I know he can do whatever he likes with me.

"I am going to ask you one final question, and I need you to be honest with me, or I will have your head." The way he threatens me bothers me, but my mouth smiles from ear to ear, like my thoughts are removed.

"Yes, my king. What is it?" I want to vomit at the performance I am giving.

"Do you know the guard from the hallway?" I know if I don't tell Pharoah the truth, I could be sent to prison, raped, or tortured. So, I bow at his feet, come up with a lie, and come up with it quickly.

"Yes, I do know him. I was afraid he would recognize me and try to become my friend again. His name is Abasi. He wasn't very kind to me when we were kids."

I look Pharoah in the eyes as I finish lying once again to him.

"So, you were concealing your identity from him?"

"Yes, I was. However, I would be more comfortable if he would leave me alone until I get to know my way around here, if it pleases you, my king."

Pharoah lifts me back to my feet, and as he does, he unties the knot at the base of my neck. After that, Pharoah is preparing to do whatever he wants with me.

"I can arrange that for you, but first, you have to let me touch you. Can your Pharoah touch you? I am not allowed to have sex with the women until the selection process is done. That would be breaking tradition and would not please the gods. And we don't want to make the gods angry, do we?"

I agree and feel the straps of my dress fall to the floor. The gown clings to my hips. It is my breasts Pharoah is interested in, and right now, all I can do is stand and let him suck each one of them. His lips disgust me, and no matter how good Pharoah is at pleasing the ladies, he will never have my heart. My heart belongs to another, and his eyes gazed upon me today, my childhood crush, my Abasi.

Chapter 8: Dr. Sawyer (Kira's POV)

Present Day:

Alex takes my hand and leads me away from Dr. Sawyer. Pretending to be someone else's girlfriend is not exactly what I had in mind. It is not what I had planned. Asher would break up with me on the spot if he could see me now. I know that he would. I wouldn't blame him. In the name of research, I got in a car with a stranger and went off to the Field Museum of Chicago in the dead of night. It is not an ideal situation by any means, but here I am enjoying the company of the mysterious boy from my university's library.

"I am sorry about my father; he gets a little excited and passionate about Egypt. I thought you could breathe some fresh air. The truth is my father believes that we can go back in time. He believes that somewhere within these old treasures is a time-traveling device. He believes you are the key to unlocking the secrets of the past. If you truly are Cleotina's descendant, you have the power to help us within your veins."

I push Alex away and still feel his lips on my mouth. No matter how sexy that kiss was, he is just speaking nonsense now.

"Alex, do you hear yourself? This is crazy talk. Humans can't go back in time; it is not possible. And even if we could, can we get back? Would it alter everything we know now? I don't want to be a part of this. I just wanted to know what happened to my ancestor and know what she did to be named the murderer of King Tut in my family. I thought we were doing a research paper, not an unscientific experiment. This is a waste of my time."

"It doesn't have to be a waste of time. In fact, my dear, we can have as much time in the world as we want if you help me translate these hieroglyphs. I know you can do it. You said it yourself that you can speak and write in ancient Egyptian," Dr. Sawyer says as he interrupts our conversation.

His presence fills my heart with utter terror, and his impulses to keep me hostage at this museum overnight for his pleasures are even harder to comprehend. He removes my cell phone and does a magician's trick to hide it from me. Now I am at their will to do whatever they want.

"No, I can't. I never said that," I say, rejecting all of this.

"But you can read Coptic, can't you," Alex asks.

"Yes, what about it?"

"That was the language was used to translate the hieroglyphs with. It was a French man named Champollion. He was a brilliant linguist at the time. If he can do it, you can do it just by looking at it."

I nod. I suppose it is possible. But under pressure from Jekyll and Mr. Hyde is enough to make Halloween come early and for the Pharaohs to rise out of their very graves. Dr. Sawyer hands me a bracelet.

"This bracelet belonged to Nebetta. A woman believed to be your ancestor's best friend. It is believed that this artifact possessed unusual properties when worn by the right person. A person who makes deals with the god Petbe may pass special powers to their descendants. If you are really Cleotina's ancestor, you will be able to unlock this power. All I need is a sample of your blood."

Dr. Sawyer takes a knife and has Alex grab me by both arms. I couldn't go anywhere, and suddenly I realized why Alex was in the university library. He was stalking me. Perhaps he had been for a while now. All because his father needed my blood for a weird alleged ancient Egyptian ritual to go back in time. I hope I can go back in time and forget this ever happened in the first place.

Dr. Sawyer takes out an old scroll and puts the wrinkled papyrus in my face. The edges are torn like thousands of hands have rubbed it over the many years it was covered by sand.

"I need you to read this. Use your Coptic and read this scroll. Then I will prick your hand with this knife. Make sure you are wearing Nebetta's bracelet. That's the most important part. Go on, my dear, don't fight us. We are historians on your side of history. Don't you want to know what happened the night King Tut was murdered? Don't you want to know if your ancestor lived or died? Was she buried alive? Was she married to Abasi, her alleged lover? Don't you want to know if her tongue was cut out or if she was buried alive with snakes? Or does she make it out alive in time?"

Alex places the golden bracelet on my wrist. It's heavy, and I can feel the wealth of Egypt extend through its finery. Dr. Sawyer opens the papyrus scroll, and the hieroglyphs emerge from the page. I can hear the spirits of the gods whisper out to me. A massive smokey cloud hovers from the scroll as my Coptic finds my lips. In English, it means:

The person who wears the bracelet of time,

Is said to be committing a great crime,

For when time is twisted, things appear,

From the ashes of dust, don't stay too near,

Don't linger too long, for if you do,

It will lead to your doom,

If you want to see the best of history,

The wearer of the bracelet must keep this power a mystery,

For if you don't, your family might die,

The Egyptian curse of Petbe is nye...

The King will gift the bracelet to his lover,

Who will kill him for the love of another,

So, beware everyone who touches this jewel,

Egypt will now open in time for you fools...

Dr. Sawyer takes the knife and pricks my wrist. A small drop of my blood touches the edges of the bracelet and falls down to the scroll. The ink in the papyrus mixes with my blood, and the truth of Cleotina is known. A ghost appears from the papyrus. A man with two giant green snakes coming out of his head looks into my eyes and calls me by name.

"Kira, descendent of Cleotina, would you like to know the truth," the god says?

"Petbe, is that you? Yes, I want to know how King Tutankhamun perishes. I want to know what happened to Cleotina, my ancestor."

Then Petbe opens up a portal with his hand and holds out his other to me. The portal twists and winds and howls like the wind. It sucks in artifacts from the museum, and as I am sensing this all, Dr. Sawyer has a twisted smile on his face. His smile tells me all I need to know that he was right. That stalking me for his own career gain was well worth it.

I take Petbe's hand, and the portal gets larger and sucks us into the vortex. The tornado of the portal spins around the room.

"Only the bracelet wearer may come into the dominion of old," Petbe says, as the two giant green snakes on his head attempt to bite and snap to keep Alex and his father away from the portal. The larger snake bites Dr. Sawyer's hand, the vipers hiss and rattle their tails.

"I knew it. I knew you were the descendant of Cleotina. Alex, my boy, I knew she was the one. We have to go with her into the past. Oh, great god, I want to bring back the treasures of long ago and study them here in my museum. I am a historian, not a treasure hunter. Will you allow my son and me to pass to this portal's other side?"

Petbe's snake continues to bite into Dr. Sawyer's arm. Alex is allowed to accompany me through the portal.

"Your son has a pure heart. Therefore, only he may be allowed to accompany the girl to the other side. He must wear a bracelet as well. Go get one, Dr. Sawyer."

Dr. Sawyer does what Petbe says and places an ancient silver bracelet on his son's forearm. Alex cuts his hand with a knife and offers his blood as payment to go through the portal. The god of revenge allows us to pass, and the wind grows louder as the snake-headed god guides us into the past.

Chapter 9: Time Travel (Kira's POV)

Traveling to the past:

My head became numb during our journey to the past, and my lips became chapped. The tornado of time twists and winds, lightning dances and flashes at its center. It is a beautiful and terrifying display of color and chaos. Alex and I are frozen in the void as Petbe grips our hands. We are but astronauts floating between the great nothingness of time and space. Purple clouds drift in and out of the dark vortex, and the wind howls as we glide through time.

I observe famous battles and famous kings from the safety of the vortex. They are entirely unaware of my presence. But I am aware of theirs. Some of them I know, and some of them I don't. Others will do great things for humanity, and others will be a curse on the world. The snakes on Petbe's head rattle and twist. They are still alive and are judging my every movement.

The vortex stops, and Petbe lets go of my hand and places it in Alex's. The tornado of purple quiets down, and the clouds disperse. A large brown door sits between our time and theirs.

"Where are we, great god," I ask because Alex is too terrified to speak? He is still in awe that his dad was right, and that time travel is still possible.

"We are here at the time that we spoke of. Go and find out what happened to your ancestor. But be aware they cannot see or hear you. The bracelets will protect you from being seen. If you take them off, I will not be able to rescue you. Stay with Alex. Learn what happened here. Find out the truth of what became of King Tutankhamun. See how his journey came to an end and how history is a stubborn fool. Meet me here when your journey is complete and recite these words to summon me.

Bracelet of time, bracelet of time,

I have learned a truth that is not mine,
I have come, and I have seen,
Bring me home, so I can redeem,
Redeem the past and a truth I now know,
Must be told for mankind to grow,
Take me home, and help me heal,
Thank you for showing me what is real."

I write the summon message down on a piece of paper and stick it in my bag. The great god takes the snakes off his head and wraps them around our bodies. The green snakes slither their coils up our legs as the great god speaks in ancient Egyptian. He changes our skin color and makes our clothes match the era we are now in.

"Be brave, Kira. And Alex, redeem your family name. Your father has dishonored the gods. So, it is up to you to clear the Sawyer name."

We both bow and honor him. The great god Petbe releases us from the snakes' grips. They slither back to their master and turn into stone on top of his mighty crown.

"I shall see you both when Pharaoh's life has ended. To get back, recite the summons and never take your bracelets off."

Alex holds my hand, and I hold his back. I should be mad at Alex for lying to me, but he is my comrade now. The only person here who knows me, the only person here who can see me.

"Petbe, how shall we eat? How shall we drink," Alex asks?

"I will prepare a meal for you every night, and you shall camp here. Don't worry about food Alex Sawyer. I, Petbe, am with you. I must go and close the time portal."

Alex waves at Petbe, who smiles and waves back. He is both terrifying and humble. If I never believed in the ancient Egyptian gods, I do now. It's all real, and it has been this whole time, waiting for my bloodline to reconnect with its ancient roots.

"It's amazing, isn't it, Kira. Look where we are. Look at what you're wearing. Wow, you're gorgeous."

A great redness comes to my face as I rush over to a nearby water source and stare at my reflection. My green eyes are brighter and are more emerald. My head covering is pink, and my dress matches.

"Thanks, Alex. I thought I was mad at you. But if Petbe thinks you can redeem yourself, maybe you can redeem yourself for me too. So maybe we can be friends after this, depending on how everything goes."

Alex smiles and heads into his tent. It's been a long night, and after everything that has happened today, I don't want to be alone. So, without asking, I go into Alex's tent and lie next to him. I grab his arm and let him hold me all night long because his arms are the only comfort I will find in the land of ancient Egypt.

Chapter 10: A Selfish Pharoah (Cleotina's POV)

Pharaoh finishes pleasuring himself with my body. My breasts are still showing as he smiles at them like he is proud of his handy work. My thoughts are still with Abasi and the glimpses we shared in the hallway a moment ago.

Nebetta is the only thing we ever had in common. Abasi and I weren't friends, but here in the land of the Pharaoh's wrath, his friendship is the only authentic one I can trust.

"I look forward to our next meeting, Cleotina. You have brought joy to my lips today. I will tell Ay of your achievement here today and see if you can graduate from the selection process sooner rather than later. Would that please you?"

Again, Pharaoh is testing me to see if I have an opinion of my own. Of course, I do, but I dare not tell him it is to rip his vocal cords out and feed him to the Nile crocodiles.

"It is not for me to say, great king. That is for you to know and to tell me only."

With vengeance on my lips, I think of Gyasi, Abasi, and Nebetta and the revenge that the Lower Egyptian nobles are entitled to. Pharaoh can have whoever he wants whenever he wants, which means he is spoiled. I must spoil him before he spoils me. I won't be able to recognize myself before my selection process is complete.

"Very good, Cleotina. You are always keeping me on my toes. One of these days, I'll get you to play along. But until then, I will see you later. So, see yourself out, and don't do anything I won't do."

I bow as low as I can and kiss his hand on my way out. I cover my face and hide who I am. My face is to be covered in a veil of shame. It is a reminder that I am no one, no one but the property of the Pharaoh. My voice belongs to him, and my thoughts are meaningless. To live is to die, and to die is freedom. The rumors of death must be true, for no sane woman would want to live out her days here fucking the Pharaoh for the glory of Egypt. It sounded like paradise to me as a child, but now I see what it is. A prison, a prison of my heart, my mind, and my body.

Nebetta is free because she doesn't have to live in this hell on earth. I will avenge her and end myself before Ay or Horemheb can have the pleasure of harming me themselves. Perhaps Abasi can be persuaded to end my life after I reveal my mission to him.

I close the door to the bedchamber as I continue hanging my head low for the cowardly Pharaoh. He is a villain, and he knows he can do whatever he wants. His charm and handsome face make it hard to hate him, but I do more than he knows.

The guards escort me back to my room. My small room, and my servant, Nephthys, await my return. She knows the king has touched me. She inspects every inch of me as she starts another bath. Cleanliness is a way of life around here. They use water in criminal amounts. Lower Egypt is thirsty, and here they bath in it for hours like they have earned the right. They are the most entitled brutes I have ever come to witness. If I ever get out of here, I will write about this place and warn my descendants of this treachery.

"Excuse me, miss Cleotina, I need to run and grab more towels. We seemed to have run out. A guard is standing at the door. I won't be long, shout at the guard if you need anything," Nephthys says as she opens the door and heads out.

I turn the water off while she's away to save it. I don't need to bask in this luxury being shown off to me.

The door opens quietly, and I hear the slight squeak of the hinges. A shadow rushes into my bathing chamber. A young guard with black hair appears before me. He covers his eyes and reaches out to touch my hand. I'm not scared because I know it's Abasi coming to check on me.

"Cleotina, is it really you," Abasi asks, risking his career as a guard by even being here? If I am going to win him over, this is my only chance.

"Yes, Abasi. It's me. I've been chosen to participate in Pharaoh's harem selection process. He wants to get me approved quickly so he can have his way with me."

"He already had that honor tonight. I thought," Abasi interrupts me.

"No, he just touched everything on my top. He hasn't spoiled me yet. Abasi, can I be forward with you? Since we are pressed for time?"

"Yes, what is it," Abasi asks while hiding his eyes. His respect for women never ceases to amaze me. It's a rarity in Egypt that a man would respect a woman.

"It's Gyasi. He wants me to avenge Nebetta's death. That's why I have come. To win Pharaoh's favor and end him. Will you help me? If I succeed, will you kill me? She was your sister, Abasi. Surely you must want to do something."

He opens his eyes, and they find mine. He looks at my naked body sitting in the hot tub. He quickly covers his eyes again.

"Sorry, I didn't mean to look."

"But I want you to look," I say to Abasi as my heart flutters and red reaches my cheeks. We both always had a thing for each other, and with my death coming near, I want to indulge in what Abasi has to offer me.

"You do? But I thought you belonged to the Pharaoh."

"I don't belong to anyone. I always wanted to belong to you. But it's too late for that, Abasi. We are here, in the land of the dead. We can indulge each other a little before the end. What do you say, will you end my life if I succeed in killing Pharaoh?"

He opens his eyes again and nods. I lean my head on the backside of the hot tub, and Abasi puts his hand on my cheek. Our lips touch for the first time. We both have always wanted to kiss each other. We just had to be in the land of control to find each other.

Abasi leaves before Nephthys returns, he guards the door, and the feeling of his lips still tingles the edges of my smile. But, if I'm not careful, my feelings for Abasi will betray me, and it could be the end for both of us.

Chapter 11: In Time with Alex Sawyer (Kira's POV)

Alex is still sleeping next to me. His breath is calm and soothing. His arms are the only thing keeping me safe in the land of Egypt. I know he tricked me into his father's plan. But Petbe, the god, said that Alex has a pure heart. I wonder what Asher's heart would be like if an Egyptian god were to read his soul. I don't have a pure heart. I don't know why I am allowed to witness the happenings of the past. Petbe is allowing me to see what really happened the night King Tut died.

Alex's arms wrap around me tighter, and I can't help but love the feeling of his warm body pressed against mine. His chest completely touched my back. Maybe I'm attracted to him a little. I turn over to face Alex and kiss his cheek. What the hell am I doing? We're here to learn about Cleotina, not fall in love.

Alex wakes up, startled that we are still lying beside each other. But it was me who followed him into his tent last night. He didn't choose that for us. I did.

"Did you just kiss me," Alex asks while rubbing the spot I kissed?

"No, I didn't. If I did, it was a mistake. I shouldn't even be in your tent. I'm not sure why I am here or what sort of arrangement you have with the Egyptian gods to make me like you, but I am here to tell you it won't work. Their voodoo may be crafty, but I have my wits about me. You haven't won, Alex Sawyer."

He gets his arms out from under my body. And turns to look at me. His dark brown eyes make my knees buckle, and his dark hair, even though uncombed, makes me blush.

"What are you talking about? I have no arrangement with Petbe if that's what you are implying. Do you seriously think I had him cast a spell on you? That's just crazy. But it is nice to know you like me," Alex says as he tilts his head toward mine.

"I do not..." Who am I kidding?

"Yes, you do," Alex replies trying to get a rise out of me. And it's working better than he knows.

"I do not. I am happily engaged to Asher. He's smart and daring. He doesn't trick me into doing his father's bidding. No, he is nothing like you. Minster Pure of Heart."

"You really need to stop fooling yourself. Asher isn't here. Look where we are, Kira. It's just you and me in Egypt. No one else here is from the twenty-first century."

"I am not fooling myself. I am happily in love with Asher, and when I return to him, we're getting married," I bark, trying to be intimating with my hands on my hips.

Alex climbs on top of me, and my face turns red. My heart pounds against my rib cage like it was always meant to be there. The Egyptian birds sing their morning song and Alex's lip brush against mine for a second. He wants to kiss me too.

All the kisses we shared at the museum were a show for his father. They were all fake, despite how amazing they felt. But this is different. He really wants something from me, and I want him to want it as badly as I do. Even admitting that to myself is a betrayal toward Asher, but Alex is right Asher is not here.

I close my eyes, and Alex's face is close to mine. I wrap my arms around his neck, and our lips touch. He opens his mouth as I close mine. My tongue finds its way into his mouth, and we can't stop what we've started. Our attraction has crossed over space and time, and even if I am thousands of years in the past, I am still cheating on Asher. But being with Alex feels real, more real than any encounter I had with Asher.

I roll over and find myself on top of Alex. He starts to take his shirt off. Something I have never seen before. His bare chest is more toned than Asher's, and he's sexier than anyone else I've kissed before. But do I really want to throw my future marriage away to be with Alex?

"I'm sorry, Alex. I can't do this. I love Asher. Excuse me. I think I need to go."

I've never cheated on anyone before. But suddenly, the guilt train pulls into the station. It won't budge, and it eats away at my soul.

Petbe appears. Did Alex summon him? The green smoke lifts from the sand and a great meal is presented before me.

"Don't cry, child. You must have patience. Patience will tell you what you must do. Patience is always on your side. It's okay to fall for another. Especially for one so pure of heart."

"Are you talking about, Alex? I don't know what to do about that."

The god transforms into a human and hugs me. His arms are comforting, and I am sure he wants something in exchange.

"Go and be with him. And enjoy the breakfast I have prepared for you," Petbe says in a soothing whisper. Then, the great god disappears into the green smoke that he rose from.

Petbe wants me to be with Alex? Is that why he brought us to the past? Not so I could learn about Cleotina, but so I could discover my feelings for Alex.

I look at the tent and sigh. I'm ashamed that I left him there. A plate of breakfast sits on a nearby rock. I pick it up and offer it to Alex as a piece offering. I return to the tent, and Alex is still in the same spot I left him in.

"Listen, Alex, I'm sorry about earlier. I got scared. I've never been with anyone else other than Asher. He and I have known each other for a long time. But with you, it's different. I don't know what I'm saying. I like you a lot more than I should. I mean, we hardly know each other, but I feel like we've known each other for a long time. Can we try again and see what happens? I'm willing to try again if you are."

Alex opens up the blanket and nods in agreement.

"I'm sorry too. I wasn't trying to push you. Maybe we can test us out a little before going too far."

I smile as I climb into the covers beside him. I let him hold me again, and we kiss a little as the sun rises higher in the sky. I'm not the best judge of character, but if Petbe wants us to be together, there must be a reason that being with him feels so damn good. For now, I will trust in that and not pull away from my feelings for Alex no matter where it takes us. I won't have sex with him now, but if that's where we end up later, then so be it.

Chapter 12: We Are Family (Cleotina's POV)

Nephthys returns to my chambers, and Abasi's kiss still exists somewhere in my heart. I wish I could confide in her, my hidden passion. But I can't. It would be an instant death sentence for both of us. Abasi is correct; however, no matter how much I want to deny it, I belong to the Pharaoh. I belong to his hands, I belong to his harem, and to love someone else besides his royal Highness is not safe.

Love is for men, and crushes are for women. Lust is for men. Rape is for women. Heartbreak is for women, and falling in love is for men. That's the way of the Egyptians. It is how it always has been.

Before my eyes close on this world, I want to tell Abasi how I truly feel about him. Although I've loved him from afar, it took his sister's execution and a forbidden kiss to solidify my affections toward the man I grew up with once upon a time in Lower Egypt.

I pray to Hathor, the Egyptian goddess of love.

"Hathor, wherever you are, please be with Abasi tonight. Let us be together once before the sunsets in our eyes."

A tear falls down my face as my eyes meet Nephthys's. She kneels beside me; her knees pop and crack as she does. She folds her hands and starts her evening prayers.

"Who were you praying to, my dear," Nephthys asks?

She has a grandmotherly presence about her that is almost soothing. She cares for me a little but not enough to spare me an execution. If Ay discovers I kissed Abasi, he will have my tongue ripped out and will make Abasi eat it. I've heard the stories of the tortures he chooses to pleasure himself with.

"No one, really. I was just praying," I reply.

"To Hathor, the goddess of love. And tell me, who is it you are in love with? Did I hear you pray for protection over Abasi, the king's guard? Now isn't that interesting."

She caught me. I don't know how she found out or when, but for an elderly woman, she knows her way around other women's hearts.

"Yes. I was praying for Abasi. Can you keep a secret?"

"Dear, this is Pharaoh Tutankhamun's palace. There are no secrets here. I let the guard in. I knew you grew up together. I won't say anything. I was like you once, kissing the palace guards in secret. My guard's name was Akins. He was a fine gentleman. I wanted to marry him, but I was Pharaoh's property. I am here to remind you that you are at a critical period in the selection process. If you severe that now there will be no redeeming yourself and no turning back. Ay, and Horemheb will have both our necks for even having this conversation. However, I will help you make your prayer come true. I will give you and your Abasi one night together of your choosing. After that one night is up, you will never see him again. Do you understand?"

My smile brightens, and my eyes turn red. Nephthys is like me, after all, a woman once in love with a man who she could never have. But she is letting me have him once, and once is what I prayed for.

"Yes, I understand Nephthys. Thank you. And Nephthys, can you pass a message along to Abasi for me?"

Nephthys bows, and I help her to her feet. She nods and holds my hands.

"We are family now, child. The harem women have an unbreakable bond. We all suffer the same fate, and that brings us closer together. I will send word to Abasi and tell him of your wishes for a meeting. You tell me when and I will make it happen. After that, you must promise me you will never speak of him again."

I agree to Nephthys's terms and know it is the best offer I will ever get. All I want is to be touched by a man I love before the Pharaoh spoils the rest of my body for the glory of Egypt.

Chapter 13: Observing the Past (Kira's POV)

Alex and I make our way to the Pharaoh's palace to observe the Egyptians of the past. The Egyptians serve Ra and His blessed son, Pharaoh. The palace walls are thicker than I ever imagined them to be. I put my hair behind my ear and stare down at Alex's hand. My feelings for him still confuse me, and my insides match my confusion.

He catches my eye, staring at our hands. I don't make a move on Alex. Even though the Egyptians of the past can't see us, I'm too shy to hold his hand in front of anyone. I could barely return to his tent a second time.

"You can hold my hand if you want, Kira. I don't bite."

The bracelets are still on our wrists and are protecting us from becoming one with this time. I hesitate to hold Alex's hand. My engagement to Asher dangles above a fire. Alex takes my hand and makes a decision we both can live with. Our fingers intertwine as I gaze upon the Pharaoh for the first time. He speaks Egyptian, which I am able to catch bits and pieces of with my Coptic.

"What's he saying? Can you understand him, Kira?"

Pharaoh stands high above his subjects, and as he lifts his hand, silence hovers within the large courtyard.

"I will do my best to translate," I reply while listening.

"He says beloved people of Egypt. The time of the selection process is almost here. Tomorrow at noon, I will announce twenty-five women who will be selected for my harem. As you all know, this task has not been an easy one. There are a few favorites among them, to be sure. I will prepare a great feast this evening to begin the celebration. After that, it will be an evening to honor the gods and pick the remaining few women. But tomorrow night, I shall select my shining star, my favorite among my favorites. She shall be the woman I will share my bed with in three nights from now. The Pharaoh has spoken, and the gods will it. Peace be with you, my subjects, and may Ra bless us during our new selection cycle."

Petbe appears before us, and the great green cloud appears.

"Petbe, can they see you? The Egyptians."

"No, I have covered their eyes with my hands. But you, Kira, have proven yourself worthy of receiving a gift. For you, I give you the power to understand the ancient tongues of the Egyptians, and the same goes for your Alex Sawyer. Ra has spoken, and I shall obey his commands. Be careful, Kira. The bracelets shall fall off at first light in three suns from now. In three days, you will know Pharaoh's fate. Go and find Abasi and follow him to Cleotina."

Petbe touches our lips and our ears. He gives us the power to understand all that is around us. Alex listens in awe of the conversations he couldn't understand a moment ago.

"Fascinating. This is absolutely fascinating. We are actually able to understand Egyptian the way we would English back home. Oh, if only my father could hear this."

Alex smiles, but the mention of his father has me pulling away.

"Be careful, Alex. Don't let curiosity distract you from your mission. I must return to Ra's banquet. He is also preparing his own selection cycle for this year. Hathor, the goddess of love, looks like a fine choice this season."

"What do you mean by the selection process, Petbe," I ask, hoping my suspicion of women being taken from their homes for the Pharaoh's pleasure was nothing more than a legend.

"Your suspicions are accurate, Kira. You would have been sent away to pleasure the Pharaoh if you lived during this time. If you don't pass the selection process, you either become a priestess, work for the Pharaoh, or are put to death by the King's advisor," Alex replies.

"He is correct, my dear. That is the way of it. But these bracelets will protect you from being selected. If they fall off, I will not be able to send you home. So, the only gift that shall remain with you is the gift to write and read in this tongue. So, stay together at all times, now go find Abasi, and he shall lead you to Cleotina."

Alex holds my hand again, and the comfort of his touch forces me to my feet. If my bracelet falls off, I couldn't be with Alex...I mean Asher.

"Thank you, Petbe. We understand. How will we know we have found him?"

"He will be wearing a blue cloak, and he will have a sword tucked on his right side. He is left-handed. And Kira, don't be afraid to follow your heart. It could lead you down a better path."

Petbe summons the great green mist and disappears before our eyes. Alex looks at me with a puzzled brow. I don't have time to answer him. Instead, I merely grab his hand and drag him through the halls of the palace.

They can't see us because our bracelets protect us. We walk through walls like ghosts. We descend deeper into the heart of the palace and find hundreds of women dressing up and getting ready for the selection banquet. Nothing disgusts me more than to see the terror on their faces. Some are excited to fuck the Pharaoh, and others are sad because they know they will die or live out their days as celibate priestesses.

"You pity them, don't you, Kira? Your face says it."

"I wish they could be with someone who cares for them. Everyone deserves that."

Alex chuckles as we continue through the various corridors.

"What in heaven's name is so funny about that," I ask?

"You wish them happiness but can't even give it to yourself," Alex replies while crossing his arms and pushing past me.

"What does that mean? I am quite happy with Asher, thank you."

"Who are you trying to fool? Keep telling yourself that," Alex replies again as his voice gets louder. An angry voice tells me I've done something to upset him, and I don't even know what.

"We are happy. We will grow old together...and... will live...a... happy life."

"Why are you holding my hand? Why did you come into my tent last night? Perhaps you deserve the same fate as these women here," Alex says as he lets go of my hand.

"Alex, no, don't. I..." The words stop, and I have nothing to give him.

Alex disappears behind the walls of the palace. He leaves me to find Abasi by myself. I can't be falling for Alex, can I? It doesn't happen that fast, does it?

The words of Petbe return to my thoughts.

And Kira, don't be afraid to follow your heart. It could lead you down a better path...

Does he mean Alex? Does he want me to be with Alex?

"Alex, where are you? Alex?"

A bodyguard with a blue cloak leans against the door I am walking through. Being ghost-like has its advantages. At least Abasi can't see me.

"I'm right here, Kira. Please stop teasing me. You're making it worse for both of us. You can sleep in your tent tonight. I will help you complete this mission, and then when it's time to go home, I hope you and Asher have a wonderful life together."

There's no time to fix what is happening between Alex and me. Abasi stands tall as the Pharaoh walks by. He bows in his presence, and I find myself bowing as well. An invisible force pushes Alex to the floor as well. We both kneel before the Pharaoh, who can't hear or see us.

Minutes pass, and we manage to stand to our feet. Abasi rises from the ground. Moments later, an older woman appears.

"Abasi, I have a message from Cleotina. You are to meet her tonight after the selection banquet. I will come to get you when the rest of the palace is sleeping. I have arranged for you both to have one night together. Don't be late. Will you accept her invitation," the older woman asks?

"Yes, Nephthys. I accept. Please tell Cleotina that I love her."

"Tell her yourself, you great fool. Do you want the whole palace to know? The things I do for young love. Come at midnight, and don't be late," Nephthys says.

Abasi leaves the hallway as Alex, and I begin to head back toward camp.

"Spirits, I know you are there," Nephthys cries to us.

"Alex, she's speaking to us. What do we do," I whisper.

"Just listen, I guess," Alex replies. My body starts to tremble uncontrollably, and my urge to remove my bracelet grows stronger.

"Kira, don't take it off. She can't hear us," Alex says with urgency.

"Spirits, listen, a great danger is coming. But, please, I beg you, let Abasi and Cleotina have one night together," Nephthys prays.

"She's only praying. Don't take it off, Kira. I can't lose you in this place. Get up."

But I can't get up. My legs are locked, and I am helpless. This woman is praying blessings over Abasi and Cleotina, and all I want to know is who to be with. I turn to Alex and see the look of urgency in his eyes. I grab his head and put it in my hands. I stroke his cheek with my thumbs in an attempt to press my lips against his. He denies me the kiss, and my heart shatters inside. My legs break free from their binding because the truth is somewhere on this journey; I have let go of Asher forever.

Chapter 14: For Ay's Pleasure (Cleotina's POV)

The selection banquet has arrived. Nephthys spent the better part of an afternoon fussing over my hair, eye make-up, jewelry, and gown. There's more to me than a pretty face, and when old age approaches me, my youth will be gone, and Pharaoh will find the next young girl to spoil. That's how it is. That's how it will always be. There is no use in wanting to change our customs. They are the way they are, and there is no use in trying to deny it. So, Pharaoh is allowed to get old and continue to have sex with whomever he wishes, whenever he wishes.

But my body will be cast aside and will only know his touch and the touch of the other royal nobles. Or so he thinks. I will be with Abasi tonight, and I will feel him inside me. He will spoil me before the Pharaoh does.

It's what I've always wanted, to be with someone I know... with someone I love. But, of course, my affection for Abasi could get us in trouble or caught. I'm sure they will check to see if my virginity is intact. That's the way of it. On the night of the selection banquet, I will be examined, felt up, and put under lock and key until the Pharaoh summons me. I do not yet know if Pharaoh Tutankhamun has selected me to be his shining star. He has other girls he is scheduled to fondle before the ceremony. I know I will be chosen, but I don't know if I will be his favorite.

Nephthys finds me brushing my hair one last time. The sun will be setting soon, which means the banquet will start and continue into the night.

Ay, and Horemheb appear in my chambers. My heart drops to the bottom of my skin. Ay snaps his fingers and points at the nearby stool. I stand when he tells me to. My body obeys him, and I don't look into the pupils of his eyes. My very soul depends on acting the right way, which is getting harder and harder.

"Nephthys, leave us," Ay demands as Nephthys lowers her head to the ground to bow at the terrifying advisor. She turns and leaves the room. But I know Nephthys will be eavesdropping to make sure I am alright. And when Ay is done with me, I am sure there will be tears.

"Well, don't you look lovely this evening, my dear. I am here to tell you two things. The first is I am here to congratulate you on your achievement. The Pharaoh has just confided in me that you have been selected to be his shining star. A fine prize, I can assure you. But I am also here for another matter. Horemheb, if you would be so kind."

Ay raises his hand and gestures to Horemheb to come toward me.

"Horemheb grab Cleotina's arms and hold her back for me. This will only take a minute, my dear. You see, there is a rumor going around that you and that guard from Lower Egypt have slept together. It is my greatest honor to check and see if the rumors are true. Make sure to hold her back, Horemheb. I don't think she will like this very much, but I know I will."

"Get your hands off me, you pigs," I say as I fight Horemheb's strength. My body doesn't belong to them. They only think it does. Horemheb puts one of his hands down my shirt and feels my breast.

"Relax, Cleotina, I am not here to rape you yet. Pharaoh will have his shining star in three nights time but after that... I can have you over and over again until your nightmares sing of me. And Horemheb can have a go at you, too, once I'm through with you. Don't you get it? You are property now-property of the Tutankhamun dynasty. So, you'd better get used to it."

I surrender to Horemheb's strength and Ay's gluttony. They've won this time. Horemheb puts his other hand down my shirt and touches my other breast. Ay lifts my dress for the inspection and smiles at Horemheb when he does. I believe Horemheb smiles back because his deep breath has a chuckle in it, and he tightens his grip on my chest.

Ay rubs his hand up my leg slowly and inserts his fingers inside me. He feels around, going deeper and deeper. He scratches my insides and makes me wet. My wetness betrays me. He thinks it's pleasure. It's disgusting. He's disgusting. They both are indulging pigs, touching women without understanding the consequences of their actions.

"I'm glad you are enjoying yourself, my dear. In due time, you will be mine. When the Pharaoh is done with you, I can also indulge in the harem women. And your wetness tells me that you want me just as much as I want you. So, your virginity is intact for the Pharaoh. Congrats, you pass the inspection, my dear. Horemheb, let her go. She has to finish getting ready," Ay says as he removes his fingers from my body and puts his fingers into his mouth to taste the bits of me, he has forced out.

They leave as Nephthys returns. She hands me a towel to clean my wetness off.

"I'm sorry, Cleotina. He's an evil man. They both are. I hope the gods discover their wickedness before the end."

"They will, Nephthys. But, because I will kill them before the end, I will kill all of them," I say as a tear falls to my cheek.

"None of that, mistress. It's almost time for the ceremony. Here's a drink to calm your nerves."

I chug the drink. I don't even know what it is. All I know is I've passed the virginity test, and I am now free to sleep with Abasi if he'll have me.

The sun has set, and the banquet commences. Ay is seated next to Pharaoh. Then Ay proceeds to escort me to my chair. His touch is a toxic hell that burns my flesh as we walk into the banquet hall.

Hours pass, and I don't eat. I watch people smile and women dance. People bow. They come and go. And still, Pharaoh smiles like all of this isn't narcissistic. Our whole way of life is built to honor the king of narcissism. Everyone present is a fool, except the people forced to be here.

Pharaoh stands and raises his hand over the crowd. They are all silent, for his word is the law.

"My dear subjects, tonight is a glorious night indeed. Tonight, I am announcing my shining star for the selection cycle. But first, let's name the other amazing women who will also be joining her in my harem. For this year's selection ceremony, I have selected the following women. If I call your name, please come forward."

He calls them all by name. The poor other women who were also duped into believing this process was honorable. There is nothing to congratulate them on. There is no meaning in any of this. Our lives are on hold. We can't be real women. We can't be wives. We are nothing more than honored whores for the nobles to fuck when the Pharaoh has had his way with us. And I get the highest honor. The honor that makes my insides scream and want to murder that bastard king I am forced to serve.

"My new shining star is Cleotina from Lower Egypt. I will bed her in three moons, and she will honor the gods with her body. We shall become one. It is spoken. It is the law. The ceremony has ended. Thanks for coming, and we will continue the festivities tomorrow with the parade in town to celebrate the lovely Cleotina's success."

The guards escort me to my chambers. I am to be a prisoner, kept under house arrest until they need me for another banquet or ceremony. The guards congratulate me. My brother, Gyasi, will be proud that I have achieved this honor because I will get to murder that bastard even faster.

Nephthys finds me and helps me take all my make-up and jewelry off. A few more hours go by.

"Mistress, it's time. I'll fetch Abasi. But after tonight, I want to hear no more about him."

I nod as she leaves. I make my hair pretty for him and quickly put on perfume. He's the real lucky man of the hour. He gets to have me before Ay or Pharaoh. I would rather die in Abasi's arms than be an honored whore.

Nephthys returns with Abasi. Abasi stands in the doorway with a flower in his hand. He gives it to me, and we both know why he is here. We don't have time to fall in love properly. We don't have time for any of those things. Our affection is enough, and our common ground in mourning the loss of Nebetta is enough.

"You look beautiful tonight, Cleotina. Are you sure you want to do this with me? Are you sure this isn't a mistake?"

"We don't have time to worry about any of those things. I love you, Abasi. I'll be forward with you about that. I've always loved you. And before the Pharaoh has me, I want you to have me first."

Abasi walks over and puts my face in his hands. He puts his forehead against mine.

"I love you too, Cleotina. Even when we were kids, you were the only girl I wanted. So, when I heard you were being selected and summoned to the palace, I was so happy to know I would see you again. I wanted to see you so I could finally tell you."

Abasi puts his lips on mine, and I pull away and smile. I kiss him back. He lifts me and puts me on the bed. He takes off his clothes and shows his nakedness to me. We don't have time to go slow. When you love someone, you love them. And tonight, I love Abasi, the actual prince of my heart.

He inserts his fingers into me where Ay's were hours earlier. His fingers don't insult my insides. Instead, his touch is gentle and soothing. His skin against mine makes me want him more. He slips my gown off and puts himself inside me. The harder he presses, the more we both want it. I put my lips on Abasi's and indulge myself in his touch for one night.

Chapter 15: Confused About Alex (Kira's POV)

Alex is still mad at me. He pushed my kiss away. I would feel like a rebound if I were in his shoes. But I've been letting go of Asher more and more these past few days. My lust for Alex is turning into feelings.

After following Cleotina through the selection ceremony and witnessing her secret love for Abasi, I now realize how lucky I am. If this time bracelet falls off, I will be no better off than Cleotina and the rest of the harem women. I would be felt up and fondled just like them. I couldn't choose Asher or Alex if I lived here.

I follow Alex back toward the camp. We left before Abasi and Cleotina got too physical. It was obvious they were going to have sex, and my ghostly presence needed to honor their only night together. Being a witness to history as an outsider has given me time to think about what is most important.

Alex goes into his tent, and before he does, he points at my tent. I know what it means. It means he is done with my emotional confusion. He is done with my engagement to Asher. He is done with me feeling anything for him. I didn't ask to go on this crazy Egyptian crusade with him. It's all happened so quickly and without warning. But Petbe, the great god, did allow Alex to escort me into this era.

I head into my tent and find an array of food Petbe has left for us. I bring a plate to Alex's tent. I leave it at his door and return to my tent. We aren't talking. He doesn't even like me anymore.

As I grab the contents of my dinner, I look at my hands. My engagement ring glares up at me. I walk out of the tent and squeeze the ring as hard as possible. It won't come off and won't budge. I pull the ring as the sweat on my skin forces it to move. It gets stuck on my knuckle, and my knuckle bleeds. But I don't care.

"Come off, damn ring. Come off...I can't...wear you anymore. Get off, now."

As I pull it, I hear Alex walking toward me. I throw the ring as hard as I can into the Egyptian sands. It lands somewhere on the dune, and the wind hides it from view. It gets quickly covered up by the sand.

"What are you throwing? Who are you talking to," he asks as he sees the blood on my hand?

"I tossed my engagement ring into the sand, Alex. I can't do this anymore. Excuse me. I need to be alone."

My shoulders shake. I've just broken up with Asher emotionally. He isn't here for me to dump. But it still means the same thing. I've cheated on him, and he deserves better than me. My face hits the pillow in my tent. Alex follows me into my tent.

"Your hand is bleeding. I can't just walk away. Let me help you with that."

I don't fight him. Instead, I let him tend to my knuckle, which had an engagement ring on a few moments ago.

"Why did you toss your engagement ring? What does that mean to you?"

"Don't you get it, Alex? I'm going to break up with Asher. You're right. I don't love him as much as I think I do. I thought I did. But coming here and being with...you made me realize... You know what, never mind."

Alex washes the wound out with water and covers it with a few band-aids he was hiding in his pocket.

"If you're wondering why I have band-aids in my pocket, I am quite the klutz. You don't have to break up with Asher on my account. Don't worry about me, Kira. When we go home, I'll return you to him, and we can go our separate ways."

I don't like the way he says, 'separate ways.' It all sounds so final.

"I don't want to go our separate ways. I want...I want you, Alex. Maybe this is all happening so quickly, but it feels right to be with you. I think I could really fall for you if I let myself."

Alex finishes putting the band-aid on my knuckle. And soon, our hands intertwine. Alex lies beside me on the bed. Our faces are turned toward each other, and he smiles at me.

"No one's ever said that to me before. I really like you too, Kira. I have for a while now. Even at university, when my father wanted me to collect information about you. I got to know you from afar, and I liked what I saw. When you were with Asher, that was hard. I won't lie. You looked at him the way you are looking at me now. And that makes me happy," Alex says as he puts his lips on mine.

Alex lies on top of me and kisses me. This is a real kiss, one we both want. I put my arms around his neck and no longer care about my engagement to Asher. I've ended it for good. Asher wasn't a bad man. He was just the wrong one for me. Petbe was right; I just needed to let myself go and trust whatever came my way.

Alex's touch is intoxicating, and just like Abasi and Cleotina, we decide to make love under the night sky of ancient Egypt. Alex removes his clothes, and I remove mine. We get back into bed, and our hearts become one. I feel him inside me like it was always meant to happen this way. Asher and I had never had sex before. Despite our endless years together, he wanted to wait. It drove me nuts, and the anticipation of getting married killed all desire.

Alex lets me explore all of him. His scent as he sweats washes over me. And I am glad that I am giving myself away to him. The deeper he goes, the louder I get. Finally, our lips lock again, and as our lips separate, I hear Alex whisper three very distinct words, "I love you." When our lips lock again, I press him onto the bed and realize that I have fallen fast and hard. And being with Alex Sawyer is the best damn feeling in the world.

Chapter 16: Ay Returns (Cleotina's POV)

Abasi leaves my chambers before the first light. In two nights, I will murder the Pharaoh. Abasi and I have made our arrangements to give Pharaoh the proper death he deserves. However, I still need to wipe out Ay and Horemheb. If I am only allowed to kill one, then Ay has done me more wrong than Horemheb. Ay has murdered Nebetta with his orders, just like that bastard king who sits on the throne.

Their deaths will be quick and satisfying. Abasi has reluctantly agreed to end me if we don't make it out in time. I have a big day ahead of me with the parade to not look forward to. There will be sacrifices to the gods today. Rumor has it Ay will have a public execution for a few women who didn't make it into the harem, temples, or servant status.

I know fifty women that have not been placed yet within the palace. They will die, and no suggestion I make will allow them to live. I could suggest Pharaoh gift them to the Nubian King. But they would only live out their days as enslaved women in a foreign country. When dying would be a better solution to everything. I would rather die than be sold as an enslaved person if I were them.

Being the favorite whore of the harem is no honor. The only honor there is is knowing Tutankhamun will die soon. Two more nights, and I can kill him. Two more nights and his afterlife will be here sooner than he knows.

The sunrise brings the orange ball into the sky. Nephthys brings me my breakfast. My wetness is still present this morning, and my legs hurt slightly from my first time with a man.

"It's time for a bath, mistress. After last night, I suggest you take one quickly and clean yourself out properly."

I do as she says, and blood pours out into the bath a little. I take the soap and scrub my skin and rub the scent of Abasi off me. If Ay can hear it all, he can smell it too. I must hide my truth from everyone for two nights. As I sit in the bath, Ay makes his entrance. He makes such a spectacle of himself. Perhaps if I indulge his ears with flattery, he will leave me alone faster.

"Good morning, my lord; to what do I owe this pleasure?"

"Cut the pleasantries, Cleotina. I am here to remind you about the fifty women whose fate now rests in my hands. It is up to you if they live or not. If you double-cross me, I will kill them all."

"So do what you like with them, my lord. They are yours to deal with, not mine. And you know I've been thinking about your proposition today. Perhaps when my night with the Pharaoh is done, I could become one of your regulars."

His smile twists with an appetite to devour me. He has tasted my body, and his lustful eyes crave all of me, for I have been named the most beautiful woman in all of Lower Egypt. I know Ay fears the gods, and he will not touch me before the Pharaoh does.

"So, you have been thinking of me then," Ay asks? I picture Abasi asking me, and that makes it easier to reply.

"Yes, I have. Does that please you, my lord?"

"More than you know, girl," he says as he reaches for my hand in the bath. He places my hand on his parts so I can feel how big he has become. I know he will want to touch some part of me this morning, and I can't risk the lower half being discovered.

I take his hand and place it on my breast. I stand up and expose my bare chest to him. His eyes burn with desire as he licks his lips. I grab his head and let him suck on my chest. He kisses every inch of them, and it feels like poison. But I have to give a part of myself to him. Otherwise, Abasi could be killed. I think of Abasi and smile. Ay sees my smile and thinks it's for him.

"Don't fall in love with me yet, Cleotina. You still have your night with the Pharaoh to look forward to. But I did enjoy our time together. And yes, I believe you will be one of my regular women to keep me company. I can tell we have a certain undeniable chemistry."

Ay leaves me in the bath. Nephthys appears with a towel. I use soap to wash away, Ay's touch. If I am to survive and succeed on my mission, I will have to be sexual with Ay every day until the Pharaoh is done with my body.

"I saw the whole thing, my lady. He is going to want more tomorrow morning. What will you do if he discovers you, and you know?"

"I will have to pleasure him, somehow. I will worry about that later. I want you to know Abasi, and I have made arrangements for our plans. And after two nights from now, you may never see me again."

"What are you two planning?"

"I am going to murder Pharaoh Tutankhamun. He murdered Nebetta, my beloved friend, and she was Abasi's sister. This mission is important to us. Do you promise not to say anything?"

Nephthys takes my hands and knows I am telling the truth. There is no other way. It must be done before I don't have the will to do it. If I overthink it, I will chicken out. And that is the last thing either one of us wants.

"I promise. I want you to know. I think of you as a daughter, my lady. You've been so kind to me. I have enjoyed our time together. So, if I don't ever see you again, please remember me. And look for me in the next life."

I hug Nephthys, and we head to the parade of hell together. In the palace courtyard are fifty terrified women. They are surrounded by soldiers who are beating them with whips. I know if I speak out, Ay won't hesitate to have me flogged with them.

Ay holds his whip, and a black-haired, olive-skinned beauty emerges. Horemheb removes her gown and reveals her whole body to the crowd. They tie her hands with rope and flog her five times. She screams in agony as her blood flies across the sky. Horemheb cuts her tongue out and then slips her throat. They do this to the next ten women.

Pharaoh Tutankhamun finds me and sits beside me. I smile at him and pretend I enjoy the torture in front of me.

"Are you enjoying yourself this morning? Ay thought you might enjoy seeing him work. He wanted me to tell you that this is the same fate your friend Nebetta endured. Isn't that ironic that she died in the same method? She was useless to me, you know. Nebetta wasn't pretty like you. I gave her to Ay, you see, and he flogged her quite a few times, if I recall. She didn't scream until the sixth lash came ripping down her back. It was a beautiful sight to behold."

Nephthys looks at me, and I remember the hairpin my brother gave me. It's in my hair now, and all I would have to do is remove it from my black hair and stick it into his neck and make him wish he had never been born. I hold it in, and Nephthys holds my hand. I squeeze her hand for support, and Tutankhamun notices.

"Have I offended you? I am just telling you the truth."

"You disgust me, sir. You and your whole council of rappers. This isn't entertainment, and it doesn't honor the gods. Nephthys, take me back to my room. I've seen enough."

"I am sorry you feel that way about me. I truly do. I thought we had a better understanding. I tell you what. You are not going anywhere. You will stay here with me and watch every single one of them rot, or you can join them. What do you choose," Pharaoh Tutankhamun asks? If I join them, then Pharaoh can't be murdered.

"You're right. I was out of line, your highness. I will stay and watch the women be put to death if it's what your majesty commands," I bow as low as I can stand it.

I want to spit in his eyes when I rise. But I know that that is not an option. I kiss Pharaoh's ring, and he forgives me. It's as if my words have been erased. He could have ended me, but he didn't, only because I am his shining star. After our sexual encounter, he may change his mind, which is why I will not back down on my promise to Gyasi. Nebetta will be avenged even if it costs me my life.

Chapter 17: Home Sick (Kira's POV)

"I can't be here anymore, Alex. I want to go home. I no longer care how King Tutankhamun died. I want Petbe to send us back. I can't watch them execute all these women. I can't stand the brutality of this era any longer. It's so wrong."

Alex puts his arms around me. Ever since we had sex last night, I don't want to leave his side. Abasi and Cleotina will never have a chance to fall in love, but Alex and I will. We already have, and as for my fiancé Asher he is nothing but a distant memory. Where I am, he hasn't even been born yet.

"It's okay, Kira. You're safe. You're with me. And you are wearing a time bracelet. They won't see you or hear you. So, rest your head on my shoulder. I will let you know when it is over."

Despite not seeing the women being flogged and beaten. I can still hear them. I can still listen to their cries and imagine what every lash whipping across their back feels like. The only scars on my own body are from stitches in my left knee when I fell off my bike at age seven. I thought that was painful, but in comparison, theirs is agony.

Beautiful foreign women are being wasted at the expense of the Egyptian nobles' amusement. The only torture I have ever seen was in movies and TV series. It was okay to watch hell on screens because it wasn't real, but this is real. It's different knowing what is real and what is fake. Reality kicks in, and the sound of the next woman's scream causes me to vomit.

"We can go. They are done now. I'm sorry we have to be here. Petbe told us to follow Cleotina. If you want to know what happened to your ancestor, the only way is by observing and witnessing the history unfolding before us, no matter how horrible or cruel this time may seem to us. For them, this is normal. Their culture and customs are strange to us, but back then, this is how it was," Alex says as he holds me closer.

"I already told you, Alex, I don't care about watching King Tut die. This is too much for me to witness anymore. I don't want to watch Ay force Cleotina to pleasure himself with her body again. I don't want to watch them hit another woman. Can we go home?"

Alex holds my hand and leads me away from the crowds of tortured women. We head back to our camp and are met by a very unlikely visitor: Hathor, the goddess of love.

"Hello, Neferekira, ancestor of Cleotina. I come with a message. I have seen the changes in your heart and a shift in your loyalty. The sands of time have spoken to me and have told me of your betrothed. Why do you abandon his trust with this man I see before me? Petbe told me that this, Alex Sawyer, is pure of heart which is rare in a man. Do you know about his bloodline?"

Hathor's red hair blends in with the black highlights. Two large horns carrying a sun disc appear on top of her head.

"What about his bloodline," I ask, now turning to Alex?

"What about my bloodline? I'm British. I am Alexander Sawyer. There is nothing special about my bloodline." Alex kicks some sand around, nervous to hear the following words of the goddess Hathor.

"Your father never told you the truth, that you are the descendant of Abasi of Lower Egypt. Why do you think you both fell in love so easily? It was not a coincidence; nothing is. Abasi's love for Cleotina and vice versa, lives in your DNA. In essence, you are their reincarnations. You are falling in love in another life. It was always meant to be," Hathor replies as she sits on a nearby rock.

"Then what about Asher? Why was I engaged to him," I ask? Of course, my relationship with Asher has to have some part to play in all of this.

"It's simple. You betrayed Asher the way Cleotina will soon betray Tutankhamun. Asher is a living descendant of King Tut."

"But King Tut had no sons or daughters. They were all failed pregnancies. So, all the babies were born dead. We know this from the hieroglyphs," Alex says, trying to understand the correlation.

"You forget that King Tut's queen is also his sister, Ankhesenamun," Hathor replies.

"What does she have to do with anything? We haven't even seen her yet. Where is this invisible sister of his?"

"During the selection process, the Queen of Egypt is always sent away so that jealousy won't get the better of her. Right now, she is on a diplomatic errand to Nubia. She won't return until the selection cycle is complete. Her beloved husband and brother, King Tutankhamun, will be dead when she returns. She will go on to marry Ay and will carry his child. That child is the closest bloodline to King Tutankhamun. It is also the very bloodline of your former fiancé. Asher is the descendant of that line. So, you see the events unfolding here are being repeated by their very own descendants through you."

Hathor may be a goddess, but I don't believe her. There is no way that we are all Egyptian descendants. It would be too coincidental. Or have the gods of Egypt always meant for history to repeat itself in an eternal dance through bloodlines until the truth is known?

"Why would the goddess of love tell us this? What does this information mean for us?"

"It means you shouldn't leave this era just yet. Continue to watch Abasi and Cleotina and learn from their mistakes before they become your own. History repeats itself, but it doesn't not all need to unfold in the same manner. So, I implore you to remain here and keep your time bracelets on for two more moons. Then, when King Tut's death is complete, come back here and summon Petbe. Then, you can return home when your mission is complete."

Hathor disappears like Petbe does, except her cloud is a blue mist instead of a green one.

Alex pulls me in and hugs me. We were always meant to be. It was written in the stars before either of us was born. I don't want to stay here, but Hathor and Petbe want me to learn something from all of this. Maybe this isn't a mission to learn about Cleotina. Perhaps I was sent on this crazy quest to know the truth about myself. If I am

Cleotina's reincarnation, maybe it is like looking in a mirror to discover my truth, that I am free to love Alex Sawyer no matter what.

Chapter 18: Remember the Mission (Cleotina's POV)

I am numb to the events unfolding before me. The women's public flogging has ended. I haven't seen Abasi since he left my chambers. I fear he has been discovered and is being held prisoner somewhere within the palace. Or perhaps he is dead.

My heart has been broken into a thousand ways today, from the sounds of the women screaming to Ay's desire to touch me. There is no solace to be found here, and the gods mock me. Being a noblewoman means nothing. Being a woman means nothing. We are born for men, but men aren't born for us but from us.

Men will end life, but they will never bring life into the world. For them, it is a race to the great afterlife beyond. The rest of the festivities happen around me. Women dance in the street, and animals march in lines as the crowds surround them. Civilians are excited about the parade that is being presented to them in my honor.

The banquet hall fills with hungry men. But the harem women have no appetite. We have lost our sisters today. We have lost our way today. Being the shining star in the harem means nothing. Pharaoh forced me to watch him murder innocent women today. In their memory, I will murder him for all the people who have been raped, defiled, and tortured. The death of Pharaoh will be for your vengeance.

The moon rises, and I retire to my room. Abasi won't comfort me tonight. Last night was our only time together. I would be spoiled if he returned. This is the last night that Pharaoh will be breathing. Tomorrow night is the night to end all nightmares. Tomorrow is the evening of my vengeance—the vengeance of the shining star who won the Pharaoh's favor. I will pleasure him a bit, and as he climaxes, I will end him with the blade in my hair. I will stick it in his throat, and he will bleed out the way Nebetta was bled out.

The murder details must be reviewed over and over again. Any hesitation or slip-up will mean I have failed at my mission. I will dishonor Gyasi if Pharaoh is still breathing in two nights from now. And worst of all, I will have failed Abasi. Nebetta might have been my best friend, but she was his sister. I am scared of failing him, the man that I love.

My chance of making it out of Pharaoh's palace alive tomorrow night is very slim. I know what the risks are. I know what failing at this mission would mean. If Ay captures me before the end, he will rape me every night until he is dead. Failing is not an option, but death is the only freedom I will have. I know that I will likely die when the mission is complete.

Nephthys helps me prepare for bedtime. She knows that this is my real last night in this room. Tomorrow I will either be dead or on the run. She gives me a drink to calm my nerves. The same one she gave me when Ay and Horemheb had their fun with my womanhood.

I lie down in my bed and try to forget what I saw today. But I can't. It's on repeat, an endless migraine of screaming. I tremble a little when I think of them—their queen of the harem trembles at their execution. No one is here to comfort me. I only have my arms to cry into tonight.

I hear feet tapping on the floor near my bed. The stars shine through my evening curtains.

"Cleotina, I am here to be with you one more time. I wanted to see you again, my love," Abasi says as he climbs into bed with me. Not even Nephthys knows he is here.

"Are you crazy? Do you want to get caught?"

"I want to review my escape plan with you. I have figured it out. I know which hallways to travel through. While everyone was distracted by your parade today, I studied Pharaoh's secret tunnels. There is a hidden passage behind the large picture hanging in Pharaoh's bedroom. I followed it and marked the trail today with small stones to the exit. We can murder the bastard tomorrow and slip out together through the wall. Then, we can run away to Nubia and leave Egypt together forever."

Abasi is clever for using the parade as a distraction to learn the hallways and passageways that I never knew existed. And if he didn't know they existed before, no one would ever suspect that he has marked the trail to our freedom.

"I must say I am impressed, Abasi. I was worried you were in prison today. But instead, you were busy studying our escape route. I was convinced I would die tomorrow night, and I have been accepting my fate all week. If we can run away to Nubia together, so be it. We can't travel on foot."

"I have already figured that out. We will take some camels. There is a stable not too far away from the palace. The tunnel exit is close to it. I have been hiding food for our journey every day. I have been stealing some grain. No one will notice that that's been missing too. We can make it, Cleotina."

We talk into the early hours of the morning. Then, finally, he leaves while the stars are still out, and I get a few hours of sleep under the protection of Petbe.

Petbe, god of revenge, protect me today, as I seek to fulfill my oath to you. Hathor, the goddess of love, guard our hearts and guide us safely across the desert into Nubian freedom.

Chapter 19: The Shining Star (Cleotina's POV)

The day passes, and as predicted, Ay enters my room, wanting something from me. I force myself to pleasure him by sucking on his part. When he leaves, vomit comes out. It's evidence that life here would ruin me and make bile come forth daily.

By noon the sun is at its highest. Pharaoh takes me to the temples where the harem rejects will live out their days serving the various gods. I wish I were one of them. But being a priestess would mean freedom. And if Abasi fails in our escape plan, I won't be allowed to choose my fate.

Pharaoh won't stop looking at me at lunch, his greedy grin widens, and his eyes look down at my chest. I finish eating the fish and some grain.

"Cleotina, now that you have finished your meal, I have decided to add a new custom to the selection festivities," Pharaoh Tutankhamun says as he stands to make a speech.

"Honorable noblemen, this is Cleotina, my shining star, and as some of you know, she spoke out against me, her Pharaoh, yesterday. So, I sat long and hard and decided that before she shares my bed tonight, the men can lay their eyes upon her nakedness. So, if all of you would follow me, Cleotina will now entertain the men in the next room."

Nephthys looks at me, and my face has gone pale. How much more of myself am I expected to give away? They won't touch me, but they will look at me and want to, which is just as horrifying. Then, finally, Pharaoh Tutankhamun takes my hand, and I pretend to smile, pretend that this is an honor.

"You look pale. You should drink water before I have Horemheb remove your gown. I'm sorry it's come to this, but you really should hold back your tongue. Don't worry. They won't touch you. They know you are mine tonight, my shining star," he says as he puts his tongue down my throat. If I bit down on his tongue, would he bleed? The temptation to end him now is strong, but I don't.

Pharaoh passes me off to Ay. Who leads me to the stool. The stool, I've learned, is like a stage for the harem women to be humiliated for the sexual desires of men.

The doors to the meeting room close, and the men gather in a circle around me. Their appetite to devour me makes me want to purge. My lunch has turned into ashes in my stomach.

Twenty men are seated and watch as Horemheb and Ay approach me. I stand there and decide to tune them all out. But it's next to impossible as Pharaoh speaks again.

"My wonderful friends, you are about to witness the beauty of my harem. My desert flower, my shining star, Cleotina. Remember my friends to look and not touch, for touching is what I get to indulge myself in later. Horemheb and Ay remove her gown."

Ay and Horemheb take their daggers and tear my gown to shreds. They cut my shoulder straps, and my dress falls to the floor. My chest is exposed, and they can all see it. Ay pulls the entire gown off my waist, and my whole body is presented to Pharaoh's closest friends. Horemheb holds my arms back and pushes my chest out. He parades me around the room and sticks my chest into all their faces so they can have a closer look.

Horemheb holds me in front of the Pharaoh. Pharaoh touches my chest and kisses my body in front of his men.

"If you gentlemen would be so kind. I think Cleotina and I need some time alone." The men leave, and Ay pushes me to the floor.

"I will have my way with you tomorrow," Ay whispers as the hair on my neck stands up, remembering our forced encounter this morning. The men all leave, and it's just Pharaoh and me.

"You have only yourself to blame, you know. Don't worry; you are still my shining star. You can still prove yourself worthy tonight. Do not fail me, Cleotina. I expect to be pleasured by you. And don't worry, I want to pleasure you as well. You'd better rest. Return to your chambers, and let Nephthys take care of you until I call upon you tonight. Abasi, escort Cleotina to her chambers. And here, use this towel to cover your body with."

I sit on my torn gown and take the towel. My eyes are red and swollen. Pharaoh is gone, and Abasi saw the whole thing. I didn't see him, but I know he was there. It was no accident that Abasi was in the room. Pharaoh wanted to make Abasi jealous and punish me at the same time. And he's won, the sick bastard.

"Come, Cleotina. Let's get you to your chambers, and we can talk there."

I manage to nod at Abasi. I follow him to my chambers. He sits next to me on my bed.

"Are you going to be able to kill him tonight," Abasi asks?

I nod. Of course, I am. The anger has festered into a giant monster, a monster of revenge. And the revenge of Cleotina is not the place for a Pharaoh to be in because it can only mean death for him.

"I love you, Cleotina. We will get out of here. Don't worry, my love. I will get you away from this, and those bastards will never touch you again."

Abasi lifts my head, and my eyes cry. I cry as Abasi finds my lips. I kiss him back and find great comfort in his kindness. Abasi gets up to leave before he has been gone too long.

"Abasi, I love you too." He smiles and holds my hand for a moment. Then, the moment fades, and I am alone with Nephthys.

Nephthys enters the room and takes me to the bath. She scrubs me off, and I don't say anything. I am exhausted, and she knows it. So, I sleep in my chambers and let myself rest before I must murder the Pharaoh and run for my life.

Chapter 20: Death of a Pharoah (Cleotina's POV)

The evening to kill Pharaoh is here at last. I can taste his last breath on my lips before it happens. Rain comes from the sky, and it means Egypt is preparing to cry for the death of a king, their beloved treacherous heartless Pharaoh.

Nephthys hides the hairpin dagger in my hair. Pharaoh will be summoning me soon. He thinks I am a virgin still, but that honor has been given to Abasi. I dishonor the gods. It's hard to believe they are all real when such cruelty exists in the land of the pyramid deserts. If the gods cared at all, they would help the poor and end the abuse, rape, and poverty. Instead, the Pharaoh would be stripped of his title, and we would all be treated the same.

My dress is aquamarine and has gold embroidering around the neckline, revealing my cleavage for the Pharaoh. Abasi knows I have to fake my enjoyment of the Pharaoh. Tutankhamun will have to enter me and experience some pleasure, and then when he is distracted, that's when I can make my move.

A knock on my door means my escort to Pharaoh's chambers is about to commence. The highest honor a harem whore can be awarded is about to unfold and end in blood. Ay and Horemheb escort me to the Pharaoh's chambers. Ay looks at my cleavage, and his eyes burn an invisible hole in my dress.

"I wish it was me who had the honor of deflowering you this evening. Such a pity I have to wait for tomorrow evening. I have already reserved your bed for the next five nights following the selection cycle conclusion. I so look forward to being inside you," Ay says as he grazes my cleavage with his hand for a moment.

He has made it obvious he wishes to fuck me senseless. I want to end them both, but I know Ay must live so he can marry King

Tutankhamun's sister, Ankhesenamun, who at this very hour is on an errand to Nubia. If Ay dies, there will cease to be a Pharaoh upon the throne. I know I am dishonoring the gods by killing Tutankhamun. But, if I kill Ay, there will surely be a backlash waiting for me in the afterlife.

My private area is tight and hurts. I don't want to be around any of these ruthless men. My legs tighten, and I get nervous in anticipation of the Pharaoh's touch. I have heard he is good at pleasuring women. If so, I might enjoy having him inside me and riding his cock. But instead, I will enjoy his death more. Nebetta's death still breaks my heart, and I must break all of Egypt's to avenge her from the grave.

The doors to Pharaoh's chambers open, and he is waiting for me. He is shirtless with eye make-up drawn around his eyes. Flowers surround the bed, and incense is burning. He is trying to create a mood. I am not flattered, but I can pretend to be.

Ay and Horemheb shut the doors. And Pharaoh opens his arms wide for me. I know somewhere nearby, Abasi is standing guard, waiting for Pharaoh's life to end.

"Come Cleotina, and I shall give you a night you will speak about for a thousand years."

I walk toward Tutankhamun, and he turns me around. He sucks my neck and puts his hands on my chest. My robe falls to the floor. He inserts his fingers into my womanhood, and my wetness comes after a few minutes. I hump his hand and let him get off from my body. He removes his belt and is now naked before me. He enters me, and our lips lock. I enjoy him a little and remember the location of the hairpin dagger. Pharaoh Tutankhamun humps me, his shining star. He closes his eyes and moans with delight.

"Cleotina," he moans my name out loud. Then, when Pharaoh isn't looking, I take the hairpin out of my hair and jam it into a large vein in his neck. I push it as far as it will go. Blood squirts out in all directions, as I knew it would. I get his cock out of my body and listen to him choke on his blood. The blood falls down his neck, and to make him quiet, Abasi appears and wraps a blanket tightly around Tutankhamun's head. I put on a new robe as quickly as I can.

Abasi pulls the large painting to the side, and our mission is successful. We run down the hallways and follow the markings through the night. The trail Abasi has made is still there. We remove the trail markings as we go, so they can't follow us. We don't talk. We hold hands and run. The camels at the end of the tunnel wait for us. Abasi helps me get onto my camel, and I follow him into the night.

Guards everywhere are shouting that the Pharaoh has been murdered. But they don't recognize us. We have covered our faces and look like foreigners. We disappear onto the horizon, toward Nubia. The gods have spared our lives, and Petbe, the god of revenge, answered my prayers.

Pharaoh Tutankhamun is dead and is in a better place now. The world is better off without him. He was a young Pharaoh, only nineteen. But even nineteen-year-olds can be cruel. Ay will be a terrible ruler, but we won't be in Egypt to endure his wrath. He can hunt us for a thousand lifetimes, but we have escaped the wrath of the gods and will live out our days away from the Egyptian sun. We have chosen freedom and are fugitives without a country. I don't need Egypt to be happy. I only need Abasi. We ride through the night and will continue to Nubia. And from there perhaps to another land we have never laid eyes upon. Now Nebetta can rest in peace, and my brother Gyasi will never see me again. But he will be proud because I kept my word.

The sun rises, and Abasi and I get off the camels for a moment. He kisses me in the morning sun, and we are both happy to be alive. We only need each other, and history will never know the truth about what happened the night Tutankhamun perished. We will take that to our graves.

Chapter 21: Learning from History (Kira's POV)

Alex and I follow Abasi and Cleotina as they ride off into the desert. I can't believe they were able to escape. I would follow them more if I were allowed. But the truth is I am not allowed to follow them. For if Alex and I don't make it back to camp in time to greet Petbe, our time bracelets will fall off at first sunlight, and we will be trapped in ancient Egypt forever with nothing but the gift of speaking ancient Egyptian to comfort us.

Alex grabs my hand, and we run toward our camp. The desert winds are stronger at night, and we are caught up in a sandstorm. We arrive at camp before the sun touches the earth, and I recite the spell that Petbe told me to speak.

"*Bracelet of time, bracelet of time,*

I have learned a truth that is not mine,

I have come, and I have seen,

Bring me home so that I can redeem,

Redeem the past and a truth I now know,

Must be told for mankind to grow,

Take me home, and help me heal,

Thank you for showing me what is real."

The great green cloud covers our camp, and the tents disappear along with the food he blessed us with. The green snakes on his head are still stone, and he smiles at the completion of our mission.

"Well done, Kira, you have learned the truth about King Tutankhamun. Now go back and set the record straight. As for you, Alex Sawyer, you have redeemed your family name. Your father will be dealt with properly. Ra, the sun god, has told me that if you wish to learn about other Pharaohs, you are free to do so. We entrust the time bracelets to you to be used at a different time. Keep them safe, and do not reveal their mystery to anyone."

The door appears, and Petbe opens it. We hug him before we enter. I never thought I would embrace an Egyptian god before, but there are things that I have witnessed that I never thought existed.

The door closes, and the stars on the other side twinkle as the vortex spirals around us. The vortex is warm, heading into the future, and Alex holds my hand. Hathor, the goddess of love, waves at us and smiles at our hands holding.

"I will see you again, Kira, the descendant of Cleotina. Alexander Sawyer, take care of Kira. You both have a bright future ahead of you."

"We will, Petbe, we promise," I reply.

"Petbe, before we go home. Would it be possible for us to keep our gift of speaking ancient Egyptian?"

Petbe laughs with a deep belly laugh. He tosses his head back and continues to chuckle.

"For completing your mission, I will grant you the power to speak the ancient tongue. You will keep it for the next time you return. Remember to keep the time bracelets a secret. They are our gifts to you. And if ever you need me, recite the summons, and I will be there."

A door appears and opens. The museum where Dr. Sawyer was left behind is still there. Dr. Sawyer is gone, and the museum has been cleaned up. It is still the middle of the night on the day we left. No one knows how long we have been gone, but we know. We know that our lives have been changed and altered for the better.

I will have to end my engagement with Asher. He will not understand why I am leaving him. But it's the right thing to do. As I take a deep sign, Hathor appears and hands me my engagement ring.

"I believe you left this in the wrong era. And don't worry, my dear, your fiancé Asher hasn't been faithful to you either. When it comes to matters of the heart, I have seen it all. I am the goddess of love, after all."

I take the ring and put it in my pocket. I will have to give it back to Asher, but it's nice to know he hasn't been truthful with me either. Hathor disappears, and Alex smiles at me.

"What will we do next, Kira," Alex asks?

I grab some paper and a pen and sit down at a nearby table. It's time I set the record straight, and the world deserves to know the truth about how King Tutankhamun died.

"I have a paper to write. It's time the world knew how King Tutankhamun died. The world needs to know the name of Cleotina, and I need to tell her tale with as much accuracy as I can remember."

"I'll leave you to it then, my love," Alex says as he kisses my lips.

I sit down and put my pen on the paper. The words flow into my essay, and I write it in two hours. Alex edits it for me, and no matter what happens, I have discovered the truth about how King Tutankhamun perished at the age of nineteen. It was not a chariot accident or hand-to-hand combat. Instead, King Tutankhamun died because he overlooked the revenge of Cleotina.

The End.

About the Author

Holly Hamilton

Holly Hamilton is an author currently residing in South Carolina. Her love of writing has led her to write many novels in multiple genres some which include romance, science fiction, historical fiction, and young adult. In her free time she enjoys drinking coffee, hiking in the mountains, and playing with her kids.

www.ingramcontent.com/pod-product-compliance
Lightning Source LLC
LaVergne TN
LVHW041544070526
838199LV00046B/1826